Praise for Red As Any Blood:

'Remember Sue McCormick's na great things. You quickly become and powerful, it's not just a page t......
Lucy Beaumont

'Sue's clever writing is peppered with witty one-liners, humorous observations and period details which add depth and richness to this fabulous story, which is full of moments that had me chuckling out loud. The dynamic between Holly and Ivy is particularly delightful, with their banter and camaraderie adding a warm, light-hearted touch.

The pacing is impeccable, with twists and turns that will keep you guessing to the very end.'
Sally Carman

'The full package; murder most foul at a Christmas party cut off in a snowbound castle, a bevy of suspects, doughty heroines to do the detecting, all surrounded by mountains of food and drink spiced with snarky theatre cross-talk. Great fun. Holly and Ivy will run and run.'
George Green

'Keen-witted and observant, Holly and Ivy find themselves drawn into investigating the murder — no easy feat, given that everyone has a motive. As Ivy observes, 'Trust me to try and solve a mystery in a house of actors.'

Charmingly intriguing as the duo eliminate possible culprits and navigate a minefield of red herrings, *Red as any Blood* also unpacks class in 1950s Britain and flutters with complicated frissons of romance. As such, Holly and Ivy is set to be a must-read series for discerning aficionados of cosy crime.'
Joanne Owen, LoveReading

'Sue McCormick's clever and playful take on the country house murder mystery is an absolute joy. The characters are amusingly familiar yet full of surprises; the story warm, witty and exquisitely written. Holly and Ivy sparkle in a theatrical tale which will surely win a standing ovation.'
Amanda Whittington

Sue McCormick made her stage debut at the age of 4, singing with her mum and dad's variety act. She has been an actor for 40 years, working all over the country on stage, TV and radio, and she has written four plays which have been professionally produced.

After an MA in Creative Writing at Lancaster, she is now focused on writing. Her story 'The Pig' was a finalist in the Scottish Arts Club Competition 2020, and her debut novel, *Small Acts of Courage*, was shortlisted for The Retreat West Novel Prize.

Born and raised in Preston, she lived in Aberystwyth then 30 years in Lancaster, before moving to a small village in Dumfries and Galloway, where her partner Mark runs the oldest theatre in Scotland.

A dedicated fan of classic whodunnits, *Red As Any Blood* is the joyous fulfilment of a long-held ambition to create her own cosy crime series.

Red as any Blood is the first Holly and Ivy mystery. Look out for the second, *Sharp As Any Thorn*, in 2026.

RED AS ANY BLOOD

A Holly and Ivy Mystery

Sue McCormick

HONNO MODERN FICTION

First published in Great Britain in 2025 by Honno Press
D41, Hugh Owen Building, Aberystwyth University, Ceredigion, SY23 3DY

1 2 3 4 5 6 7 8 9 10

A catalogue record for this book is available from the British Library.

Published with the financial support of the Books Council of Wales.

This is a work of fiction and no resemblance to persons living or dead is
intended or implied.

ISBN 9781916821323 (paperback)
ISBN 9781916821330 (ebook)

Cover design by Lynzie Fitzpatrick and Mad Apple Designs.
Typeset by Elaine Sharples
Printed by 4edge Ltd

For Mark

DRAMATIS PERSONAE

Dame Elspeth Hollanby (Holly) – actress and National Treasure
Ivy Earnshaw – her dresser
Esme Arden – musical theatre star
Andrew Fergusson – Esme's husband, owner of Black Gairy
Ishbel Fergusson – Andrew's daughter from his first marriage, student
Godfrey Clifford – actor
Dorothy Drake – starlet
Elliot Mayhew – songwriter/performer
Sonya Stirling – film star
Max Coyle – Sonya's husband, press tycoon
Ben Newman – playwright
Donald MacRae – caretaker
Jean MacRae – his wife, housekeeper
Fiona MacRae – their daughter, student

BLACK GAIRY

GROUND FLOOR

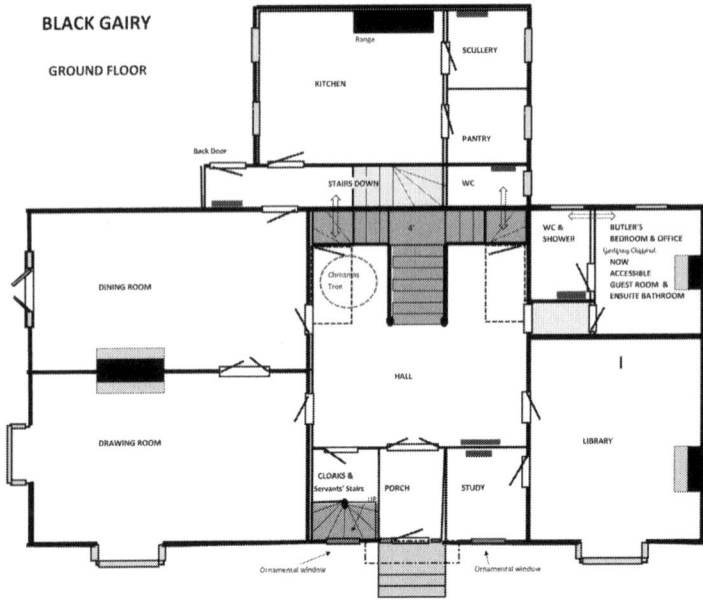

FIRST FLOOR

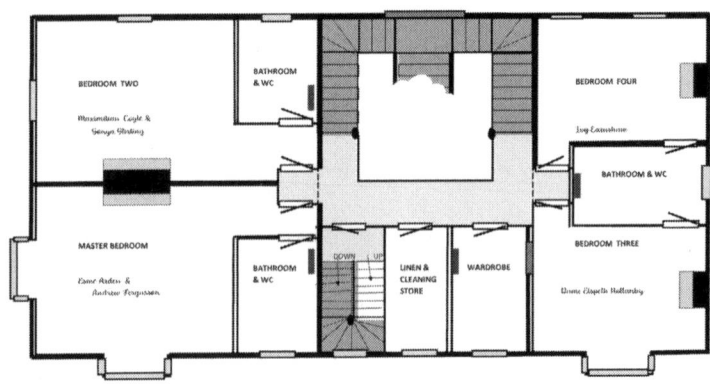

SECOND FLOOR

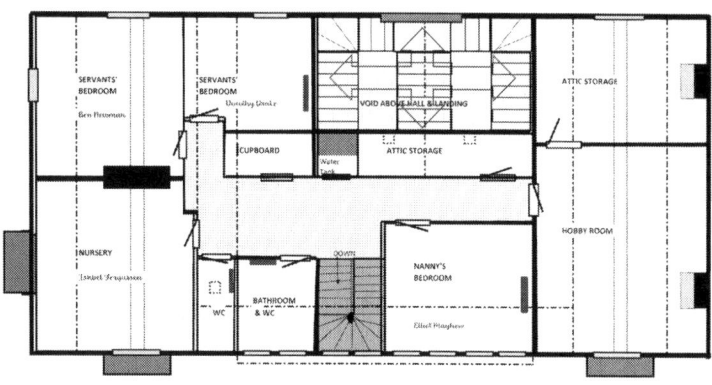

BASEMENT

1

IVY

I went because Holly asked me for help and I'd never let her down. I was in two minds about it though, to be honest. I could say it was a foreboding of what was to come, but it wasn't. I don't believe in all that guff.

The thing is, I've always spent Christmas at my mum and dad's. Every year, without fail. Even though my job takes me all over the shop, I've always made it back home for the big day, for the paper trimmings and singsongs, the silly hats and Mum's plum duff. It's family, isn't it? And it works out well because, since the war ended, Holly – my boss – has gone abroad in December. She's often too busy for a summer holiday so she blocks off a few weeks at the end of the year and gets away to somewhere exotic with her latest admirer while I head home to the glamour of Morecambe – an arrangement that suits me just fine.

I say 'boss', but Holly's a lot more than that. Dame Elspeth Hollanby, to give her the full honours, is a shining star of stage and screen, a national treasure – and a right handful. And I'm her dresser.

If you don't know much about the theatre, you'll assume I help her get her costumes on and off and, yes, I do that, but there's a lot more to it than frocks. Assistant, secretary, chauffeur, bodyguard, chief cook and bottle washer – if the cap fits, give it here. And on her side of the arrangement, Holly's like a second mum to me. Ever since she gave me the job ten years ago, we've been joined at the hip.

Except at Christmas. Even this year, when she changed her routine and accepted an invitation from her friend Esme Arden to stay at a swish house in Scotland, the plan was she would go on her own.

'Just the Fearsome Four, darling. Esme, Godfrey, Elliot and yours truly. With Esme's new husband and his daughter, at his ancestral pile in the Galloway Forest. By all accounts it's a gem. Arts and Crafts. All stained glass and wood and handcrafted tiles. It's on the shores of a lake – or loch I should say. Just the thing for Christmas. It might snow. How lovely!'

So we were all sorted. Until over coffee one morning last week, Holly threw a spanner in the works.

She was wrapped in a silk housecoat, her blonde hair still tousled from sleep. After handing me a steaming cup, she sat cradling her own, traces of last night's make-up smudged under her bright blue eyes. She's known for those eyes. They can hold oceans of grief or joy, blaze with anger or passion, keep audiences spellbound. Fixed on me across the kitchen table, they were unusually serious.

'What's up?' I asked.

'Esme called. Christmas has become a little complicated.' She took a sip of coffee. 'You know she's just done a film with Sonya Stirling?'

'Yes?'

I was instantly all ears. Sonya was a Hollywood legend and I'd been a huge fan for as long as I could remember. I'd watched her in film after film from the cheap seats in the Morecambe Odeon, loving the strong-willed, wise-cracking women she played, envying her green eyes and tumbling red hair.

'Well, you know Esme and her big heart. She asked Sonya for Christmas because her husband was out of the country for the season, although I would have thought that's a bonus, when your husband is Max Coyle.'

'And then?' I asked.

'You guessed it. Max came back and muscled in on the invitation and the upshot is, poor Esme's perfect first Christmas in her new home is to be blighted by the ghastly man.'

All I knew about Sir Maximilian Coyle was that he owned newspapers, had a lot of political influence and was rich as Croesus. He was very right wing, so I despised him on principle but that was the limit of my knowledge.

'Is he really so awful?'

Holly frowned.

'His scandal rags have destroyed many a decent person. He'll use anything to sell papers. I'm sure Esme is very anxious about letting him into her home. She didn't say as much but I could hear it in her voice.'

'So what's the plan?' I asked. I never doubted she had one.

'I suggested she expand the guest list. They have room for more and it would make things less intimate. Take the strain off a little. She needs the troops to rally behind her.'

'Are you going to take Vincent?'

She leaned back and sighed.

'I'm afraid not, darling. Vincent and I have come to the end of the road.'

'Oh, Holly.'

'It's perfectly fine. It was a mutual cooling off. No hard feelings.'

'But a whole year and a half. Was that a record?'

'I think it was.' She threw back her head and laughed. 'No wonder I was getting restless.'

'Have you got a substitute?'

'Unfortunately, no. I hadn't thought to put an understudy in place.'

Her eyes twinkled with mischief. She'll be sixty on her next birthday – a sore subject – but she has the face of a naughty child. And great actress or not, and though I love the bones of her, I knew her too well to be fooled. I put down my cup and folded my arms on the table.

'Out with it.'

'What?' She was all innocence.

'Whatever it is you're working up to.'

'Oh, very well.' She gave me one of her winning smiles. 'I was wondering if – hoping that you might come with me.'

'Me?'

'Who else, my darling?'

'We never spend Christmas together.'

'I know. All the more reason to do it this year. We could drive up over a day or two – have an adventure.'

Quick translation: I could drive four hundred miles while she chatted and dozed in the passenger seat, suggesting a refreshment stop every half hour, if past experience was anything to go by.

4

'Will it be all right with Esme?'

'Of course. She loves you.'

I knew I was making excuses. Truth is, I'm a bit resistant to change. Always have been. And then I thought, *Come on lady, get a grip. You're thirty-one and you've never spent a Christmas away from your family. And when will you get another invite like this one? A beautiful house in the wilds of Scotland. Posh frocks and cocktails. Something different, Ivy. Why not?*

That's when Holly dropped the bombshell.

'The thing is, I know it sounds dramatic but I think Esme is frightened.'

I stared at her. 'Frightened of Max Coyle?'

'Sounds silly, doesn't it? But I think so.'

It might have sounded silly from somebody else, but not from Holly. I don't know whether it's years as an actress that's honed the skill or whether she's always had it – one of the things that makes her so good at her job – but she can read people like a book. It's almost instant and she's rarely wrong. I've tried hiding my feelings from her on more than one occasion but she sees right through me. It's uncanny.

'I'm going to keep an eye on her, of course, but I'd rather not do it alone. Max Coyle is not a man to antagonise.' She reached across the table and took my hand. Her smile was uncertain, which was a rarity. 'No one does moral support like you do, darling. Will you help me?'

Everything else fell away. Holly needed me and that was the bottom line.

'Course I'll come,' I said.

So, two minds or not, that was how I found myself behind

the wheel of Holly's Bentley Continental on the day before Christmas Eve, with Her Dameship next to me and the road to Galloway stretching out for long miles ahead of us.

*

We broke the journey halfway, stopping the night in Morecambe, me at Mum and Dad's little terrace, Holly at the Midland Hotel on the prom. She invited us all to dinner there, an early Christmas meal in the restaurant overlooking the bay, dark water shifting under an expanse of starry sky and the outline of the Lakeland Hills on the horizon.

Mum and Dad were all smiles, loving the stares and whispers that follow Holly wherever she goes, basking in her reflected glory and the rare dose of glamour. Holly was attentive and charming, apologised for stealing me away at Christmas and said nice things about me, which they lapped up and which I committed to memory so I could remind her next time it was useful.

I loved seeing them get a bit of excitement, a bit of luxury. Like most working people, they haven't had it easy. Two wars in their lifetime, a general strike, a depression. No welfare state to help until a few years ago. For once they were living it up and having the time of their lives. They've always known how to enjoy themselves, given half a chance, and Holly was cutting no corners. We had a great night.

Back at home, Mum kicked off her best shoes and leant back in her chair next to the fire whilst Dad made the bedtime cuppa.

'That was lovely.'

'Wasn't it?'

'She's a good woman, Dame Elspeth. Are you still happy in the job?'

It was time for the usual questions. Every time I came home.

'Very happy.'

'It's long hours.'

'Aye, but I don't mind.'

'She pays you well?'

'She does.'

Then there was the pause and the look into my face, the little smile full of love.

'And you're not lonely?'

'No, Mum.'

'There's no one, then?'

'No.'

'It's been ten years, Ivy.'

I went over and crouched by her chair, putting my hand over hers, saying what I always said.

'You don't need to worry about me.'

'I'll always worry about you. I'm your mum.'

Maybe I should have told her there was something. A what? A possibility. A man I hardly know. Something hovering, just out of reach. How could I tell her that?

I gave her a kiss on the cheek.

'I'm fine,' I said. 'I like my life.'

Why wouldn't I? That night I slept in the room I shared for years with my sisters. Three single beds with matching eiderdowns and a memory in every corner. Then in the morning,

I put on my new sage green dress and coat and a cheeky little hat and drove to the hotel to pick up Holly. It was Christmas Eve, the winter sun was shining, the air was crisp and we were off on an adventure. I'd been to Glasgow and Edinburgh and even once to somewhere way up in the Highlands when Holly was filming, but I'd never turned left into Dumfries and Galloway before. New territory. That was the plan, Ivy.

Holly settled down in the passenger seat, swathed in French blue cashmere.

'Ready?' I asked.

'Yes, darling. The Esme Arden defence league, all present and correct.'

'Off we go, then.'

'What's the route? Go on. Do your memory thing.'

I obliged her, as usual.

'We take the coast road to Bolton le Sands, pick up the A6 through Kendal into the Lake District and onto Penrith, then Carlisle. Then the A74 to the border and Gretna, the A75 to Dumfries and the A712 to New Galloway and on to Newton Stewart, where we take the A714 to Loch Trool.'

'From one look at a road map?'

'Aye.'

'You're a prodigy.'

'Behave.'

Holly exaggerates. But I do find it easy to remember stuff. It's been my party trick for years. You know that game where you have random objects on a tray and you look at them for a minute then close your eyes and list what you remember? Every time I played it with my sisters, I won. It drove them mad that they could never beat me, no matter how much stuff they piled in front of me. Holly often says it's a shame I'm not on the stage because learning lines would be a doddle.

'There's a bit more to what you do than a good memory,' I tell her, and she alway laughs.

'Acting? It's just shouting every night in the dark. Learn the lines and don't bump into the furniture.'

She might make light of it but I know what it means to her. Nearly forty years at it and she's still addicted.

Delving into a pocket, she produced a paper bag and waved it joyfully in my direction.

'Chocolate limes?' I asked.

'What else?'

Sweets were back on ration after the lovely few months last year when they were freely available, but somehow Holly had managed to get hold of our favourites for the trip. The bag was empty before we reached Carlisle.

'Don't worry, darling,' Holly reassured me. 'I have back up supplies in my suitcase. The readiness is all. Not that we'll be short of treats at Black Gairy, I'm sure. Esme tells me the estate farm is a fountain of plenty and huge feasts are planned. She's throwing everything at this Christmas. She says Andrew is used to making more of Hogmanay, as the Scots do, but he's given her carte blanche this year.'

We were just over the border. The country was open, with views across fields to the Solway Coast, a glistening silver line in the distance. But as we turned inland, the road narrowed. Low stone walls on either side were spotted with pale lichen and carpeted in bright green moss. Beyond them, fast flowing streams broke into white foam over rocks and tree roots. The land became wilder and lonelier as we drove towards the hills and into the forest.

'It's beautiful.'

'Yes,' said Holly. 'Are you glad you came?'

'I am.'

'So am I.'

'Shame about Vincent, though. I was beginning to think, maybe he was The One.'

'Oh no, darling.' I saw the past flit across her eyes before she looked up. 'I've had The One.'

'I know. But I thought maybe it was time for another.'

'Apparently not.'

'I'm sorry.'

'It's fine. I'm fine.' She glanced across. 'And may I just say at this point, the phrase that springs to mind is "pot, kettle".'

It was my turn to remember. Sam's honest face. His young body and warm arms. A different life. A different me.

'But, unlike you...' The twinkle in her eyes was back. 'I decided to put a toe back in the water.'

'A toe? More like full body immersion!'

She hooted, wiping her eyes with the back of her manicured hand.

'Life is for living, Ivy, my girl.'

'So they tell me.'

'Speaking of which,' she added lightly, 'I believe Esme has invited Ben Newman.'

All right, if I'm honest, my heart missed a little beat. But no way was I giving Holly the satisfaction of seeing it.

'What does that mean?' I said, staring ahead at the road, deadpan.

'He likes you. I've seen it in his face.'

'Behave.'

'And you like him. Don't pretend otherwise.'

'Stop it.'

'The moody playwright. Out with French windows and in with class struggle. Don't tell me he isn't your type.'

'You got Esme to invite him, didn't you?'

'I told you she needed more guests.'

'Bloody hell.'

'Don't be like that. Where's the harm in a little romance?'

'It's embarrassing.'

'Nonsense.'

'Promise me you won't meddle,' I demanded.

'Ivy, my darling—'

'If you don't promise, I'll turn this car around right now.'

She threw up her hands. 'Very well. You win. I'll be as good as gold.'

I didn't believe her for an instant. Then again, would it really be that awful if Ben Newman was interested in me? The butterflies in my stomach said otherwise.

'Oh look!' Holly sat up in her seat. 'It's snowing.'

Light flakes were floating past the windscreen, too few to settle on the ground but by the look of the dull, sunless sky there were more to come. Hopefully we'd be parked up before then.

The road climbed and dipped for miles with fir trees towering over us on both sides, twenty, thirty feet high.

Between them, saplings sprouted in the undergrowth among dry winter ferns and scattered pine cones.

'No shortage of Christmas trees.'

We rounded another bend and both of us gasped in delight. Through a feathery snowfall, we looked down on Loch Trool curved between high hills, the rocky peaks and the water below lit by the pale sky. The valley glimmered like the inside of an oyster shell. I stopped the car and we both sat staring for a long moment. Even Holly was lost for words.

'I feel like I'm inside my gran's snow globe,' I said at last.

'Magical.' Holly pointed to a gabled roofline in the trees. 'There's the house.'

It was only yards from the loch, hidden by woodland and sheltered by the hills. There was no other building for miles.

'What a setting!'

'Let's get down there, darling. It must be gin o'clock.'

I put the car into gear and we moved off. The snow was dusting the dark trees like icing sugar. Holly started singing 'White Christmas' and wound the window down to catch snowflakes on her gloved hand.

'Max Coyle can go to hell. We're going to have a lovely time, darling,' she said. 'You'll see.'

2

Sonya Stirling was sitting at the dressing table of her luxurious guest room within the red sandstone walls of Black Gairy. Outside the window, the gloaming was settling over Loch Trool, turning the greys to mauve and darkening the trees to silhouettes. There were no stars, with the clouds low and heavy, but now and then the moon broke through and lit up the glen in a brief silver glow. The hills and the water were held in that deep stillness, that particular magical quiet that comes with the sure promise of snow.

Unmoved by the beauty of her surroundings, Sonya ran a brush through her lustrous red hair and watched her husband fitting gold studs into the starched cuffs of his evening shirt. With his back to her he was unaware of the hostility in her green eyes, but had he turned and looked at her, it would have been no surprise to him. He had seen it all before and he didn't care. Their mutual dislike was all they shared now.

Sir Maximilian Coyle was so rich and so powerful, could have so much of whatever he wanted, that ennui hovered constantly at his shoulder and any conflict was a welcome diversion. He sought it out everywhere. It amused him. That was why he had pushed his way into this Christmas house party. His wife didn't want him, their hosts were her friends, not his, and the other guests were known adversaries or wary strangers.

His reputation preceded him and it was formidable. He prided himself on that. He had clawed his way to where he was by sparing no one. Winning was everything. And if he had a few mice at the mercy of his cat's paw this Christmas, it only added to his satisfaction.

Sonya transferred her gaze to her own reflection in the dressing table mirror. The face that was her fortune was still beautiful, still lit with wit and intelligence. Her body was long and sensuous, her legendary glamour intact. She could have anyone she wanted. What was she waiting for?

'Are you ready?'

It was more a command than an enquiry, thrown over his shoulder as he walked to the door. Sonya had finished but she was damned if she was going to dance to his tune.

'Not yet. You go down.'

He left without another word. The room seemed lighter without him. Sonya regulated her breathing, stared into her own eyes and made herself a promise. It would all be over soon.

3

HOLLY

As we made the last turn in the long, tree-lined drive and pulled up in front of the house, the great door was flung open and there was Esme, fair hair caught back in a loose chignon, a floaty dress in rust and gold billowing around her like a fall of autumn leaves. She ran down the short flight of stone steps to greet us and I was barely out of the car before I was enveloped in a bear hug.

'Welcome, welcome! I'm so happy you're here!'

She turned to Ivy and gave her the same treatment.

'How was the journey? Was Holly high maintenance?'

'What do you think?'

'Nonsense,' I said. 'I was a delight.'

Esme laughed and gave me another hug. She was radiant, the most beautiful woman I've ever known, and that's saying something in my world, full of girls who go on the stage because they're too pretty to stay at home. She looked exquisite, as pale and wispy as a Botticelli goddess, as if a soft breeze would carry her away. In truth, she was born in a trunk, grew up in a touring song and dance act and emerged as tough as old boots. I've loved her for years.

Letting me go, Esme checked we were alone and lowered her voice.

'I'm sorry the original plan went awry. I would never have asked Sonya if I thought for a second that we'd be landed with her awful husband.' A shadow crossed her face but it was gone in an instant and she turned to Ivy with a smile. 'Though every cloud has a silver lining. We get you as well.'

'It's lovely to be here, thanks.'

'I'm just happy to see you, darling,' I said heartily. 'It's been much too long.'

'It has.'

'But if you will go on extended honeymoons with handsome new husbands...'

'I know. I'm incorrigible.'

'Did I hear my cue?' A smiling Andrew Fergusson came down the front steps carrying a woollen wrap which he handed to Esme. 'It's snowing, darling. Hadn't you noticed?'

'Too excited.'

He shook his head in mock exasperation and they exchanged a quick little look of love, which warmed my heart. Esme has never been lonely, if you catch my meaning, but she waited a long time to find Mr Right and I was so happy for her. He was clearly besotted. Apparently he saw her in a show, fell head over heels and wooed her for a year before she agreed to say 'I do'. I don't know what she was waiting for. Rich, cultured, handsome and charming, at fifty-five he gave her twenty years but there was nothing staid about him, even in his Harris tweeds with a pipe in his pocket. We had only met once before, at their wedding, but his manner was relaxed and there was warmth in his bright blue eyes as he greeted us.

'Welcome to Black Gairy. Quite a trek, isn't it? Blame my

grandfather. A lifetime in the Glasgow shipyards gave him a taste for isolation. But let's get you inside. You need to be by the fire with a stiff drink in your hand.'

'Come on, you two.' Esme took both our arms. 'Andrew will sort your car and luggage.'

'I can help,' Ivy offered.

'Thank you but there's no need.' Andrew smiled. 'I have reinforcements. Donald and Jean from the gate lodge are kind enough to step into the breach when required.'

'They look after the place when it's closed up,' Esme added. 'We'd usually fend for ourselves, but it's a big party this Christmas so it's all hands on deck.'

'In that case, thank you.' Ivy handed over the keys.

'In you go,' said Andrew. 'The snow's getting heavier.'

The porch had been swathed in festive greenery. The double doors were framed by stained-glass panels, their deep jewel colours echoed in smaller panes across the top of the mullioned windows on either side. The square bays towered two storeys high, their surrounds cut from deep rose sandstone flecked with gleaming quartz. The twin gables were crenelated and, between them, a row of small-paned casements sat under the eaves of the slate roof. The mottled pink and grey of the stonework gave off a warm glow, even on a snowy afternoon. It managed to be both grand and cosy, flamboyant and satisfyingly simple at the same time.

'It's a heart-stealing house.'

'Wait till you see inside. Honestly, I can't believe my good fortune. As if it wasn't more than enough to find Andrew. Then he pulls this out of his hat!' Esme laughed. 'Sorry. I know I'm disgustingly smug, but I can't help it.'

17

'I'm glad you're not taking it for granted.' Ivy turned, spreading her arms to the loch and the tree-covered hills beyond. 'All of this. It's a privilege, isn't it?'

Ivy's a political animal. She has her particular way of looking at life and we're all used to it. Actually, I agree with her much of the time, though we come from very different worlds. I was brought up to be all things ladylike and make a good marriage. Neither of which came to pass incidentally, but that's another story. Back to Ivy. She's given me an education, but it didn't stop me teasing her.

'Watch out Esme – she'll nationalise the place, given half a chance!'

Ivy grinned. 'Come the revolution!'

'She's absolutely right, though. It's such a gift. That's why I wanted you all here to share it.' Esme pushed open the doors and ushered us in.

The hall opened out and up in an expanse of pale oak panelling and eau de nil paint. There were garlands of leaves and berries on the walls and on the carved bannisters of the central staircase, which rose to a small landing then divided right and left to a galleried first floor. Beside the stairs, a vast Christmas tree sparkled like fairyland.

'Blimey,' breathed Ivy.

'Hasn't she done well?' An arch voice floated down from above. 'Did she marry the man or the house? And do we care?'

Elliot Mayhew stood looking over the gallery rail. As he spoke, he detached himself and came down to greet us. He'd been forty for a good few years now but carried it well. Slim and elegant in a sleek tuxedo, one of the new Pierre Cardin's, if I was not mistaken, Elliot was famous for being languid and witty at the piano and could be good company when he behaved himself.

'Merry Christmas, my dears.'

'Merry Christmas, Elliot.'

We both accepted a kiss on each cheek.

'Holly and Ivy. How perfectly festive.' He turned to Esme. 'Is that everyone now? Can we pull up the drawbridge and start drinking?'

'Cocktails in half an hour, my pet. Yes, it's a full house now. I'll show these two to their rooms, give them a chance to catch their breath and then we're off!'

'I shall pace the drawing room in anticipation, like Mariana in the moated grange.'

'Look, here's Dorothy. She'll keep you company.' Esme motioned to a young woman at the top of the stairs then back to us. 'Have you all met?'

I recognised Dorothy Drake, the latest graduate from the Rank Charm School. Every inch the starlet, she negotiated her descent in perilous heels with perfect poise. Her blonde hair was sleek, her make-up flawless and her dress left nothing to the imagination. It was only when she was up close that I realised how very young she was and caught the uncertainty behind her practised smile.

'No, we haven't,' she replied to Esme. 'But of course I know Dame Elspeth.'

'And the legendary Ivy Earnshaw,' added Elliot. 'The power behind the throne.'

'Ignore Elliot,' said Ivy. 'Pleased to meet you.'

'And you.'

19

'I haven't seen your debut yet.' I took her outstretched hand. 'I hear you stole the picture.'

'It's kind of you to say so.'

'She's going to be a huge star,' said Esme.

'Working with Hitch now,' Elliot drawled. 'He likes a blonde, doesn't he?'

A faint flush rose up Dorothy's pale neck. She understood the insinuation but wasn't sure how to respond. I gave her hand a squeeze.

'He knows talent when he sees it.'

We were all aware of Hitchcock's foibles and, let's face it, he wasn't alone in them. Girls like Dorothy have always suffered unwanted attention. It's bad enough we turn a blind eye, without mocking them for it. Ivy gave Elliot one of her looks and he raised an eyebrow, but then he stepped forward and offered Dorothy his arm.

'Forgive me. I get waspish when I'm thirsty. May I escort you to the drinks table?'

For a second, she looked to me, as if for guidance. I was moved. I gave her a nod and released her hand and she allowed Elliot to lead her away.

'We'll see you shortly,' Esme called after them.

I was relieved to see them chatting amicably enough as they moved out of sight.

'How old is she?' I asked Esme once we started up the stairs.

'Nineteen.'

'And young with it. Despite the glamour.'

'She seems a bit lost,' said Ivy, putting her finger on it, as she often does.

'My agent – her agent too – you know, Dickie? He asked me to invite her. She has a week off from filming at Loch Lomond and is a bit stranded.'

'No family?'

'Not within reach. Anyway, we wanted to swell our numbers and she's very welcome. Andrew's daughter, Ishbel, is home from University, so she has someone near her age. I hope she settles in.' We had turned right on the stairs to reach our rooms. 'Here you are, my dears. Make yourselves at home.'

She showed me into a large room papered in a rich William Morris pink with an expanse of bay window looking out over the lawns and trees to the loch. In the side wall, a door opened into a Jack and Jill bathroom shared with Ivy. Beyond it, her room had pale furniture and duck egg blue walls, with a view of woods and hills rising at the back of the house.

'Oh, Esme, this is lovely!'

'I'm so happy you're here.' She gave me another hug. 'I'll leave you to get settled. But don't be too long. I expect Andrew is stirring the martinis as we speak.'

She bustled off and, with my suitcases successfully delivered to the ottoman at the foot of my bed, I set about unpacking. It never takes me long. The touring life has honed my skills. I changed for dinner and was at the dressing table, attending to my face, when Ivy came in through the shared bathroom, giving the door a cursory tap as she passed.

'I could have been in flagrante with a footman!' I protested.

'Nothing I haven't seen before. Is this dress all right?'

It was midnight blue taffeta, full-skirted and calf-length with a scooped neckline and three-quarter sleeves. Her only adornments were a short pearl necklace and earrings and a matching clip in her dark curls. She looked effortlessly chic and I told her so.

'I wasn't sure where to pitch it. I've got fancier but I thought I'd save that till Christmas dinner.'

'Quite right.'

'Let's have a look at you, then. Give us a twirl.'

I stood up and displayed my dress and bolero in silver grey satin. At my neck and wrist, I had my mother's diamonds and, on my feet, my favourite Roger Vivier jewelled pumps.

'Gorgeous. Ready for the undercover operation, then?'

'Yes, darling. Max Coyle will do no harm on our watch.'

She waved an arm at the door. 'After you.'

'Just a minute.' I turned back to the mirror and checked my lipstick. With Dorothy Drake's youthful perfection still clear in my mind, I frowned at my ageing face and sighed.

'It seems no time at all since I was nineteen. Where did the time go?'

'Having a luxurious life, doing the job you love and getting worshipped for it?'

Ivy can always bring me down to earth.

'Thank you for that.'

'You're welcome.'

'Ah well,' I said, 'with mirth and laughter, let old wrinkles come. Shall we mingle?'

4

Ishbel Fergusson was sitting on the edge of her bed staring at the wall. She was all dressed for dinner and it was time to join her father and his new wife as they welcomed their guests. There were famous people to meet, stars of stage and screen. Esme Arden had brought a whole new world to Black Gairy and it was exciting, Ishbel acknowledged that. But she didn't get to her feet.

She liked Esme and was grateful for her father's new happiness. Relieved, too, that the responsibility of his loneliness was lifted from her. She had enough to deal with in her own life. Loving Jack. Closing her eyes, she lost herself in longing for a few bitter-sweet minutes. How perfect it would be if they were here together, sharing the festivities. Instead, they were miles apart, smiling and pretending and keeping their secret.

'Just a few days,' she told herself. 'This too will pass.'

She opened her eyes again. The birds in the strawberry thief wallpaper looked back at her unblinkingly.

'Let's get on with it,' she said to them.

She stood up, smoothed down her black Chanel dress and went to join the party.

5

IVY

By rights, I should still be in Morecambe, working at the library, walking home through the salty air, lighting the fire, getting the tea and waiting for Sam's key in the door. That was the life mapped out for me. A small life, but a good one.

It's fair to say my life is bigger now. I feel bad saying it because it sounds like I'm not sorry Sam died and that's far from the truth. When his ship went down, I wished that I'd drowned with him in that freezing sea. I didn't want to go on. It didn't matter that thousands of people were going through the same thing, that there was grief on every street. Nothing mattered to me but my loss. We were childhood sweethearts, married barely a year. And then he was gone and I was lost. I couldn't envisage a day when I'd be glad to feel the sun on my face, glad to be alive.

My mum was worried sick about me. She tried all sorts to take me out of myself, to get me functioning again. None of it worked. I was six months into my downward spiral when she dragged me to the Alhambra Theatre one rainy Monday night, because the visiting company from London needed extra dressers for *Lady Windermere's Fan*. Holly was playing Mrs Erlynne and she had a lot of costume changes. The rest is history.

I've changed over the years. I've grown. Or have I just got older? I don't know. Would a life with Sam have been better than the life I have now? I can't say. All I know for sure is that the me I am now wouldn't fit in the life I had then.

I mean, the drawing room at Black Gairy was about as far from Morecambe Library as you could get, but there I was, and I was happy as Larry. Yes, it was luxury and money, and I always want to spread that about more fairly, but it wasn't titles and butlers and all that stuff, it wasn't about class. It was show business – the lucky end, for sure, but still a world all its own.

The room was big. There were sofas, chairs and tables and a grand piano and it still wasn't overcrowded. A huge inglenook fireplace took up most of one wall, its wooden surround carved with intricate flowers and leaves. Great logs blazed in the cast iron hearth, lamps and wall-lights glowed and the tall bay window, its drapes drawn back, looked out on the front lawns thickly covered in white snow. It was bloody lovely.

We were the last to arrive, much to Holly's delight. She loves to make an entrance.

'Here they are!'

Esme was with Andrew, dispensing drinks at a table in the corner. She looked stunning and carefree. So far so good.

All eyes turned in our direction and Holly went into full performance mode, bless her. She was working the room before I got through the door. Leaving her to it, I accepted a drink from Andrew and had a good look around as I sipped it. I won't lie, I was searching for someone in particular.

He was standing by the window, looking out at the falling snow but, as my eyes found him, he turned, looked back at me and raised a hand in greeting. My breath stalled. No point denying it.

Ben Newman. Dark-haired, dark-eyed, quiet, with none of the glamour that was so plentiful in the room around us, but he drew me in, and I thought Holly was right, that it might be mutual. Which was a good thing, surely? Sometimes I thought it was, sometimes it scared me to death.

He wound his way across the room to join me, and my urge to stay battled my urge to run, but just as he arrived, Holly made the decision for me, appearing at my elbow as if by magic, waving an empty glass.

'Ben, darling, be an angel and get me another drink, then sit with me and tell me your news.'

He nodded and headed off. Holly sat herself down and patted the cushion next to her. I stayed standing and glared at her.

'You promised.'

'I know, I know, but I saw you about to turn on your heel and I couldn't help myself. Come and sit, darling. I'll be as good as gold. Trust me.' I snorted at that but she didn't turn a hair. 'Cynicism is very unattractive. Look, he's coming back. Sit down and give him a smile.'

I took a seat on one side of her and Ben on the other. He was carrying a cocktail shaker and gave us all a refill of ice-cold martini. It was my second in ten minutes, was very strong and didn't help my struggling powers of concentration.

'I hear congratulations are in order.' Holly raised her glass. 'An extended run for your marvellous play. You must be thrilled.'

'I am,' Ben admitted. 'Surprised but happy.'

He had caused a sensation by making the story about the working class. Lives that had rarely been of interest on stage before shown as complex characters with all their hopes and dreams and struggles. At first he was called angry, coarse, even dangerous, but full houses soon silenced his critics. Bums on seats. You can't argue with that.

'Times change and theatre must do the same,' said Holly.

Ben smiled wryly. 'Hold that thought till they see the next one.'

'Ah. I am forewarned.'

Whilst they talked, I tried to think of something intelligent to add to the conversation, failed miserably and gave up on myself in disgust. Ignoring Holly's pointed looks, I gazed around the room, taking in the other guests.

Godfrey Clifford was sitting in an armchair by the fire. With Esme and Elliot, he made up Holly's Fearsome Four, all friends for many years, in and out of work. He was wearing a green velvet smoking jacket and had his silver-topped walking stick propped beside him. Every inch the stately old man of the theatre, with his mane of white hair swept back from his brow, Godfrey had played every classical lead, from Romeo in his youth to Lear in old age. These days he limited himself to scene-stealing cameos in films from Ealing and Pinewood. 'Bank-raids', as they're known in the trade. He was worth every penny.

My eyes popped out of my head when I realised who was behind him, leaning on the mantelpiece with a glass in one hand and a cigarette holder in the other. I was totally spellbound to see her standing a few feet away in all her glory.

'That's Sonya Stirling!' I turned to Holly.

'Ah, yes. I must go and say hello.'

And off she went, leaving me and Ben side by side on the sofa. Which was what she intended all along, of course. Fortunately, I was so taken up with Sonya, I forgot to be self-conscious.

'She was my idol, growing up. I loved her films.'

'Look at you,' Ben teased. 'Completely star-struck.'

I was. For a few minutes I felt fourteen again, staring up at the screen in awe and wonder. And there was the object of my admiration, in a halter-neck pantsuit, auburn hair falling over her bare shoulders, greeting Holly with a kiss on the cheek.

'I was just thinking how much my life has changed.'

It wasn't like me to share my feelings so openly. Maybe it was the excitement. Maybe it was the martini. Either way, I regretted it right away and my awkwardness, which had been briefly missing, was back in spades. I stared into my empty glass, conscious of his eyes on me. When I finally looked up, I caught a softness in his gaze that made my heart turn over.

'It's a long way from my life too,' he said simply. 'I'll always be a trespasser in this world.'

'Why?'

'East End Marxists aren't too thick on the ground here, are they?'

'Neither are northern librarians.'

All of a sudden, I was at ease with him. My changes of mood were leaving me breathless but exhilarated. *Steady on, Ivy*, said the voice in my head. *Slow down*. But I didn't want to.

'Then again,' I said, 'it might be very grand and prosperous, but there's all sorts here. What they've got in common is success and, in most cases, talent. So get your feet under the table, lad. You've earned it.'

His laugh was warm and wry and self-deprecating.

'But do I want it?'

'Ah. Well, that's a different question.'

'I've got comrades who'd despise me for being here and enemies who'd call me a champagne socialist – not without justification.'

I shook my head. 'It isn't about not having champagne though, is it? It's about wanting everybody to have it.'

'That's right.'

The look he gave me then left me a little bit dizzy. Or was it the martinis? Before I could decide, we were interrupted by Esme calling from the drinks table and we both turned to look.

She was standing with her husband and a young woman who, I realised, must be Andrew's daughter from his first marriage. She was long-limbed, like him, and elegant in a little black dress, her dark hair held back with a comb and diamond studs sparkling in her ears. She stood at Esme's side, smiling pleasantly at the room full of strangers, doing her bit as host family with good grace, but something about her made me suspect that given the choice, she'd rather be somewhere else. I felt that Ishbel Fergusson was presenting a face.

'A quick word, my dears.' Esme held her glass aloft. 'A toast to welcome you all to Black Gairy. Andrew and Ishbel have shared their wonderful home with me and now we share it with all of you and wish you a Merry Christmas.'

'Merry Christmas,' we all chorused back.

I gave Holly a quick smile and saw that Sonya Stirling, standing behind her, wasn't focused on Esme and her family. Instead, she was staring towards the window with a taut expression, somewhere between fury and exhaustion.

In the bay, outlined against the dark glass, Dorothy Drake and Max Coyle were standing together, just too close. His hand on her arm, just too familiar. The man himself. I'd seen photographs of him but had never seen him in the flesh, as they say. It seemed particularly apt in his case. He was well-built, well-dressed, well-groomed and well-fed. Intelligent eyes and a sensuous mouth. An air of entitlement. I didn't like what I saw.

Looking back to Holly, I caught a glimpse of Andrew Fergusson and realised that I wasn't alone in my reaction. He was watching Max with contempt and anger as plain as day in his handsome face. I turned back to see if Max had noticed.

Still with his hand on Dorothy's arm, he met his wife's eyes across the room and smiled. It was knowing and cruel. Sonya turned away.

'He's a bastard,' said Ben quietly.

'You saw that?'

'Tip of the iceberg for Max Coyle.'

There was an edge to his voice. More than anger at what we'd just witnessed. Something personal.

'What is it?'

I put my hand on his arm without thinking. For what seemed a long moment, we just looked at each other. My heart thudded in my chest.

'I don't like sharing a space with him. If I'd known he was on the guest list, I wouldn't have accepted.' Then he paused and smiled. 'Who am I kidding? I wouldn't have stayed away. Not if you were here.'

There it was. Out in the open. Much sooner than I'd expected. I knew he was waiting for a response, that he deserved one, but now it was real, I had no idea how I felt. Panic, mainly. I let go of his arm like it was red hot and he looked at me as if I'd slapped him.

Esme called out again. 'Time to eat.'

There was general movement as the double doors behind her were opened. 'It's help yourself tonight. Just fill a plate and sit where you like. We'll be more formal for Christmas dinner tomorrow.'

We were the last to follow on. I couldn't find a word to say. I looked at Ben across the ocean that had opened up between us. No, not ocean. Desert.

'Better go in,' he said, and walked away.

*

The dining room was nearly as big as the drawing room. There were eleven of us and the table easily had room for more. It ran right down the centre of the room. On the left, a glimpse of French windows behind heavy tapestry drapes. Another fire crackled in another carved fireplace. Dark wood, deep red wallpaper and candlelight. More perfection.

Filling the far wall was a monster of a sideboard, laden with food and wine. Glazed ham, cold chicken, game pie, dressed salmon, cheeses, salad, fruit tarts and a beautifully iced Christmas cake in pride of place.

'Don't you have rationing in Scotland?' asked Elliot in amazement.

'We have a farm, my love,' said Esme.

'Did you kill everything on it? This is more food than I've seen in years!'

'Preparations have been underway for some time.' Andrew laughed. He had escorted both Holly and Sonya into dinner and sat between them, chatting happily, whenever Holly let him get a word in edgeways. 'I believe Jean hoarded our rations whilst we were away on honeymoon. But there's no shortage of fish and deer in these parts.'

'You'll meet Jean and Donald soon enough,' said Esme. 'And their daughter Fiona is home for Christmas and helping out too. They did most of this.' She waved at the groaning sideboard. 'But Andrew caught the salmon and I made the cake.'

'She bakes now?' Holly addressed the ether. 'Is there no end to her talents?'

'And iced it too.' Esme laughed. 'Every inch.'

'It's all wonderful.' Sonya gave Esme a dazzling smile. She was composed and charming but she never once looked across the table, to where her husband was sitting with Ishbel. 'Thank you both for your hospitality.'

'I'll second that.' Holly raised her glass. 'Here's to the Fergussons. Long life and happiness.'

We all drank the toast. I sneaked a look at Ben and felt guilty and foolish. He seemed fine, listening to Elliot telling one of his stories as he cleared his plate, which was a good sign.

'You could do much worse, my dear,' said a quiet voice at my side. Godfrey Clifford looked at me over his glass of red wine. His eyes, under bushy white eyebrows, were clouded with age but they were wise and kind. 'Forgive the obtrusion. Not my place, I know. But I am very fond of both of you and it seems such a waste of youth, not to seize the opportunity.'

'Is it so obvious?' I was surprised and embarrassed.

'Only to those who sit and watch unnoticed. Observation has been my trade for sixty years now. I'm good at it.'

'Clearly.'

'I'm sorry. I've angered you.'

'No. I'm not angry. I don't know what I am, to tell you the truth. I'm all mixed up.'

Godfrey nodded. 'Can I tell you a little story?'

'I'm listening.'

'When I was your age, I met the woman I should have spent the rest of my life with. I didn't know it at the time. I was too busy, too caught up in my career. I let the affair end with little regret, and yet she never really left my thoughts. I carried her with me. And when, years later, I realised I loved her, it was too late. She had married someone else and was lost to me.'

'I'm so sorry.'

'It was a long time ago.' He laid his old hand on top of mine, age-spotted and wrinkled, long fingers bent with arthritis, a thin wrist protruding from a spotless white shirt cuff. 'I know you have loved and lost, my dear, and I don't presume to know your heart. But you have time to find happiness again.' Mischief twinkled in his eyes. 'And it just might be sitting across the table from you, eating cold chicken and salad.'

To my horror I had to blink back tears. Because I knew he

was right, but I couldn't do it. Ten years and I was still carrying Sam with me. Even though he wouldn't want that. He'd want more for me, like I would for him. But it made no difference. I couldn't move on. I was stuck.

I gave Godfrey a watery smile. I didn't tell him what a lost cause I was. I didn't want to disappoint him. Luckily, I was rescued by Holly, who leaned across the table, waving her napkin to get our attention.

'Godfrey, darling, can I steal Ivy away? Sonya wants to meet her.'

'Of course.'

I felt a rush of blood to the head. Sonya Stirling? Bloody hell!

'Two minutes,' I said to Holly. 'Comfort break.' It was a line we'd picked up in America. I squeezed Godfrey's hand and looked him in the eye. 'Thank you.'

'You are very welcome.'

I headed for the downstairs cloakroom I'd seen earlier. The hall was in semi-darkness, lit only by the sparkling Christmas tree and a small lamp on the telephone table. That's why I didn't notice Ishbel Fergusson was on the phone until I heard her speak.

'I miss you too. I love you. Sweet dreams.'

She replaced the receiver and turned. When she saw me, she looked stricken, as if I'd caught her with her hand in the till. I pretended not to have seen it.

'I'm looking for the cloakroom,' I said, though I knew where it was.

'It's that door there.'

'Thank you.'

I left her to recover her composure. What was that about? A few sweet nothings. No harm there. What was she scared of?

Inside the cloakroom, I looked in the mirror at the face I was about to present to Sonya Stirling. I checked my mascara. It had survived so far. But the night was still young. Christmas at Black Gairy was turning out to be quite a ride. Be careful what you wish for, I supposed.

'Blimey, Ivy,' I said to my reflection. 'As my nan always said, it's a fine life if you don't weaken.'

6

The decanter of whisky was emptying rapidly. Wrapped in a silk Paisley dressing gown, Elliot Mayhew sat in the armchair next to his bed, drinking and smoking, as the snow fell outside and settled thickly on the window ledge against the leaded glass. It was the early hours of Christmas morning but there was no sign of peace and goodwill in his face. His thoughts were bitter and his eyes bright with malice. Stubbing out his cigarette, he lit another one immediately, scowling through the smoke, the spent match still dangling from his slender fingers.

Seeing Max Coyle walk into the drawing room had shaken him. Elliot had no idea he was on the guest list, might well have refused his own invitation had he known. All through drinks and dinner he had felt those mocking eyes on him, felt diminished, felt the guilt and fury rising in him like magma. It had taken every ounce of his self-control to carry on as normal and not give himself away, but long years of practice had paid off and he was sure his struggle had gone unnoticed. For now. He poured himself another drink and stared into the amber liquid, fear clutching at his heart with cold fingers. That was the question. How long could he play-act? How much more could he endure? With enough pressure, even the strongest dam will burst in the end.

7

HOLLY

'Wake up! It's Christmas!'

I took the short route through our shared bathroom and popped my head around Ivy's door.

'Wake up, sleepy head!'

She stirred and opened her eyes.

'What time is it?'

'Six thirty.'

'Middle of the night!'

'It's Christmas Day and the snow is deep and crisp and even.'

I drew back the curtains. It was still dark and the white world outside shimmered like magic in the starlight. Somewhere downstairs a light was on and a shaft of yellow lit a path to the garages and outbuildings clustered under a clump of tall pines. Beyond them, the hills rose behind the house like sentinels. Everything was covered in a heavy quilt of thick snow.

'Just look at it.' Ivy sat up to see out of the window. 'And they say there's even more to come. '

'Can we get out?'

'Do we care?'

'Not today at least. Merry Christmas, darling.'

'Merry Christmas.'

'Come through to my room. I've got the kettle on.'

Of course Esme had provided a tea tray. We drank Brodie's Edinburgh blend and munched shortbread fingers, watching in wonder as the dawn broke over the loch. I was curled in a deep armchair while Ivy spread herself on the chaise, facing the view.

'This is lovely.'

'It is.'

Outside, the wide sky lightened as night gave way to day, the snow clouds above the hills backlit with soft pink and gold. The stained-glass panes in the bay window took turns to blaze with colour as the morning sun caught them, casting rainbows on the wooden floor beyond my chair. Ivy leaned back against a needlepoint cushion and let out a long sigh of contentment.

'I could get used to this.'

'They've struck the perfect balance, haven't they? Luxury but no stuffiness.'

'That's what I was thinking last night. No butlers and silver service malarkey. I'm glad. I'm not sure how I'd cope with that.'

'You'd be absolutely fine, my girl. You're not easily awed.'

'Except by Sonya Stirling,' she laughed. 'Did I make a complete fool of myself?'

'Nothing she hasn't seen before.'

'That doesn't reassure me!'

'You had a nice little chat about the weather and the house.'

'Bloody hell!' Her face was a picture of woe. 'Worse than I thought.'

'Don't worry. You can make up for it today, engage her on current affairs and the Red Scare in Hollywood, and all will be well.'

'Funny, ha ha. Any more tea in that pot?'

As I obliged, she stood and walked into the bay, right up to the glass, looking down on the front lawn and what would have been the path to the lodge if it wasn't buried in snow.

'I like Andrew,' she said, over her shoulder. 'I'm glad for Esme.'

'Me too.'

'Why hasn't he got a Scots accent?'

'That's an expensive English education for you. Actually, he didn't grow up here. It was his grandfather's house till the mid-twenties, I believe. He's spent most of his life elsewhere.'

'But his business is in Glasgow?'

'Strictly hands off, according to Esme. Others run it for him.'

'And he just spends the profits?'

'I'm afraid so, comrade.'

'Behave.'

I cast my mind back to the night before, when we all gathered for the first time. I was keeping an eye on Esme and so couldn't help but take in Andrew too.

'He isn't enamoured of Max Coyle, did you notice?'

'Couldn't miss it. And he's got company if you ask me.'

'You felt it too?'

'There is an atmosphere.'

I felt a little nugget of disquiet lodge behind my ribs. Was I giving in to melodrama? I can be guilty of it, though I would admit that to no one but myself.

Ivy peered through the glass more closely.

'That must be Jean and Donald,' she said.

From my chair I could just about see a man and woman trudging their way up to the house, muffled against the weather.

'Coming to help with breakfast, I expect.'

'There's quite a facing from last night too. I helped Esme clear some of it before we came up but it's a big houseful to deal with.'

'Their daughter will help too, of course. And I believe a young girl from the village is joining the fray today to produce Christmas dinner. But we can all pitch in where needed.'

'Suits me. Much better than being all *Forsyte Saga*,' Ivy said.

'All what?'

'You know. The Galsworthy books. About the posh family.'

'Sorry, darling.' I shrugged. 'Haven't read them.'

'They're all ladies' maids and debutante balls and finishing schools in Switzerland. Like your life before you got famous and bohemian.'

'Am I bohemian?'

'With knobs on.'

'How delightful!' I enjoyed the idea for a moment before wagging my finger at her. 'But I have to correct you. I never went to Switzerland. I convinced my parents that I could learn elocution and deportment at drama school instead, so I was allowed to go to Central.'

Ivy raised an eyebrow. 'They knew not what they did.'

'Oh, they never dreamt I would actually go on the stage. They expected me to marry well and forget all the nonsense. Ironically, they would have got their wish with bells on if Tom had lived.'

'Really? You'd have given it all up?'

Ivy returned to the chaise. She sat cross-legged, teacup in hand and stared at me in surprise.

'In a heartbeat,' I said.

I was twenty-five, just embarking on the work that is now my lifeblood and though I loved it even then, I would have left it for him. I'd have been Lady Elspeth because of his title instead of the one I earned for myself. Running our grand house and having our children, sitting on committees, doing good works and entertaining the County. With him. A lifetime with Tom.

'Makes you think, doesn't it?' Ivy said quietly. 'By rights, neither of us should be here. But we are.'

'Do you believe in fate?'

'No.' She smiled at me. 'Just happy accidents.'

'Very happy.' I took a risk and broached the forbidden subject.

'I do wish you'd let Ben Newman sweep you off your feet.'

She was looking into her cup and didn't raise her eyes, but I saw the flush in her cheeks as she spoke.

'That's what Godfrey said to me.'

'Did he? Bless him.'

'He told me about his lost love.'

'You're honoured. He doesn't share it with many people.'

'It's sad.'

'More than you know. They had a daughter. He only found out when she was grown. They were just getting to know each other when she died.'

'Oh no! What happened?'

'I don't know the details. It was a long time ago.'

Ivy paused before she looked up with a wry smile.

'Ben tried to sweep me off my feet last night. Well, I think he did and I made a right mess of it.'

41

'Oh, darling.'

'I don't think he'll repeat the experience.'

'He will if he's serious. And I think he is, I really do.' I assumed my no-nonsense face. It works with her occasionally. 'The question is, are you?'

I saw my words had landed. She was quiet for a moment then shook her head.

'I don't have an answer to that. Sorry.'

My heart went out to her.

'I just want you to be happy, darling.'

'I am happy.'

'Happier, then.'

She put down her cup and gave me a grin.

'In that case, is it present time?'

Reluctantly I accepted that the subject was changed.

'Very well. I yield upon great persuasion. For now.'

'Do you want this or not?' She produced a large parcel tied with satin ribbon and I succumbed in an instant. Inside was a cashmere wrap in heather shades of dusty pink and mauve, with a Celtic knotwork clasp in silver and amethyst. Suitably Scottish and beautiful.

'I love it, darling. Thank you. I shall wear it today with my lilac two-piece. It's perfect.'

My gift to her also celebrated our trip north of the border. It was a first edition of Robbie Burns' collected poems. Ivy loves books, especially old books. Her face shone with delight when she realised what it was.

'Oh, Holly. Too generous.'

'Nonsense.'

'I love it. Thank you.'

Just then, a clock chimed the hour on the landing outside.

'That's eight o'clock. We should be going down for breakfast.' I jumped up. 'Bags I shower first.'

'Well, don't take forever.'

'I'll be swift.'

Ivy leaned back against the cushions and made herself comfortable.

'I've heard that one before,' she said.

*

Despite Ivy's scepticism, we were downstairs within half an hour and headed straight for the dining room where we found Esme, busy with breakfast dishes at the sideboard.

'Good morning.' I gave her a kiss. 'Merry Christmas. Can we help?'

'Merry Christmas, my dears.' Esme was radiant in slacks and a moss green twin set, a silk square the colours of seawater tied loosely at her neck. Whatever her problem with Max Coyle, she was hiding it well. But that's performers for you. Too good at pretending. She smiled at both of us. 'Did you sleep well?'

'Like an inebriated log, darling. Now, what can we do?'

'Is there more to come through?' Ivy asked.

'Yes, please. Ishbel is in the kitchen. She'll load you up. Holly, will you set some mats and napkins?'

We were soon all ready. The last dish to arrive was a steaming tureen of porridge, brought in by Jean. Esme introduced her. She was a little bird of a woman, with iron grey hair and keen blue eyes in a lined face. I wished her 'Merry Christmas' and she smiled warmly, replying in a glorious, broad accent, on the verge of unintelligible. After she left, I shot Esme a questioning glance and she laughed.

'That was "enjoy your breakfast" in Glaswegian.'

Andrew, who was building up the fire with a practised hand, looked round from the hearth.

'The MacRaes are Clydeside people. Donald worked for my father at the shipyard for forty years. We offered them the lodge when they were wiped out in the Blitz.'

'They lost two daughters in a direct hit.' Esme shook her head. 'I can't imagine.'

'How terrible.'

'Fiona is all they have now. She's their pride and joy.'

'She's a fine girl.' Andrew joined us at the buffet. 'She's reading Law at Glasgow. Won a scholarship to go. She's sharp as a pin.'

'Isn't Ishbel at Glasgow too?'

'Yes. Different department, though. It's a new thing called PPE.'

'The elements aren't new.' Ishbel came in with Ivy, just in time to elaborate. 'Politics, Philosophy and Economics are old hat. Putting them together is the recent thing.'

'I'd love a course like that,' said Ivy. 'Lucky you.'

It was obvious that she was not just being polite and Ishbel looked at her with new interest. A little of her reserve fell away and we got a glimpse of the girl we hadn't seen yet, the independent Ishbel, her version of herself away from Black Gairy.

'It's challenging.' She smiled. 'Lots of reading. Lots of debate.'

'You're describing Ivy heaven,' I said.

'She's right. Tell me more about it. I'll just grab a bowl of porridge.'

Ishbel did the same and in no time, they were heads together at the table, deep in conversation.

'I'm glad to see that,' Andrew told me quietly. 'Ishbel's been at a bit of a loose end this Christmas.'

'We invited her boyfriend but he couldn't come.' Esme was piling her plate with sausages and black pudding. Where she puts it all is a mystery, she looks like she lives on fairy dust. 'It's such a shame he isn't here. I think they're quite serious.'

'Not that she tells us anything, of course. We've never met him. Is there haggis?'

'At the back, my sweet.'

'Ah, yes.'

'Haggis for breakfast?' I asked in amazement.

'Perfect with a fry-up. Try some.'

'That's why we're eleven at table.' Esme dropped a fried egg into the last small gap on her plate. 'Jack was to make us twelve. She misses him, I can tell. It's lovely to see her chatting away. I thought she might chum up with Dorothy but they don't have much in common.'

'Dorothy seems to have chummed up with someone else,' murmured Andrew as we took our seats.

'You noticed that too.' I tried the haggis and he was right. Delicious.

'Max does it all the time,' said Esme. 'He's vile.'

There it was, the note of fear. But this time I could see it in

45

her eyes as well. Something was threatening her peace of mind. Or someone.

'Why does Sonya put up with it?' I asked.

'I have no idea.' Esme's serene face was suddenly hard as flint. 'But he won't betray her under my roof. I'll make sure of that.'

As if on cue, Dorothy made her entrance, squeezed into a powder blue woollen dress that hugged all the right places. She was carefully made up but seemed a little pale and listless. Too many cocktails last night? Or a guilty conscience? I wasn't sure. From what I saw, the chumminess was mainly on Max Coyle's side.

As if to prove my suspicions, she saw him in the doorway behind her and moved to stand by the French windows, where the drapes were drawn back, framing a snow-laden patio and lawns rising beyond it to the tree-covered hills.

'It must be a foot deep,' she said to no one in particular.

'Much more in places, I'd say.' Godfrey's voice came as a surprise. He was sitting in a wing-backed chair, facing outdoors and partly obscured from the room. 'Oh, I'm sorry, my dear,' he added as Dorothy started. 'I didn't mean to make you jump.'

'It's all right. I didn't see you.'

'Neither did I,' I called from the table. 'How long have you been hiding there, Godfrey? Can I get you anything?'

'Some more coffee would be lovely.'

'I'll get it,' Dorothy offered.

I saw her check where Max was before she approached the sideboard. He was already sitting at the end of the table and seemed oblivious to any undercurrent. Maybe I was letting my imagination get the better of me. It wouldn't be the first time!

But I didn't imagine her hand shaking as she carried the coffee to Godfrey. The cup rattled in the saucer and she had to use her free hand to steady it. Something was unsettling her and I was sure it was Max's presence. Once again, my protective instincts were roused. Someone else to watch over. As the old Chinese curse says, 'May you live in interesting times.'

'Come and sit by me, Dorothy.' I indicated the seat next to me, well away from Max and she accepted.

'I have been sitting here, contemplating this view, for about an hour.' Godfrey answered my question belatedly. 'My room is just across the hall so I strolled over at first light to commandeer this chair.'

'You're on this floor?'

'An age-related benefit, Elspeth dear.'

'There's a small room behind the library.' Esme had cleared her plate in record time. 'It was the butler's pantry in the days of Andrew's grandfather. I thought it would save Godfrey the stairs.'

'Much appreciated.'

I noticed Ivy's ears prick up. 'There's a library?'

'On the other side of the hall.'

'Can I see it after breakfast?'

'Of course you can,' said Esme.

'That's it,' I said. 'We'll never see her again. She'll move her bed in there.'

Ivy laughed and brushed a stray curl from her forehead. I thought how much her cherry red sweater suited her and that she looked very pretty.

Ben arrived, casual in an open-necked shirt and sports jacket, his dark hair unruly, a notebook and pen protruding from a top pocket, every inch the non-conformist. I sensed Ivy's awkwardness and remembered what she'd told me about last night, but he greeted everyone quite naturally, including her, and before long, she relaxed and joined in the conversation around the table. As the meal proceeded, I saw the glances he cast in her direction. He didn't have the air of a discouraged man. I was beginning to hope Ben Newman could be the unstoppable force to Ivy's immovable object. What joy!

'Am I the last?' Sonya came in, resplendent in a soft bronze dress that screamed Dior. As Esme got up to greet her, she gave us the famous charming smile. 'I'm sorry, but the bathtubs are too seductive.'

'Not that it matters a bit, but no. Elliot hasn't appeared yet.' Esme steered her to the buffet.

Sonya passed her husband on the way but neither of them acknowledged the other. There were troubled waters in that marriage, for sure. Not that I'd ever understand what Sonya saw in him in the first place. I suppose he had a kind of powerful charm and he wasn't bad looking, but he was much too fond of himself. Money, of course. Tonnes of it. But surely there was more to Sonya Stirling than that?

'Ah. Speak of the devil,' I said as Elliot appeared in the doorway.

He looked his usual urbane self but I recognise a filthy hangover when I see one. I hadn't realised he had drunk so much last night but he must have tied one on to be suffering so severely this morning. He sank into a chair and waved a limp hand in greeting.

'Morning, campers. Merry Christmas and all that.'

'And to you, darling,' Esme called across to him. 'I'll bring you some food. What would you like?'

'Just coffee. Buckets of it. Am I late?'

'Not at all.'

'I was listening to the news. Have you heard?' We all looked at him blankly. He perked up at the attention and smiled triumphantly. 'Oh, glorious! I do love to be the bearer of sensational snippets.'

'Cough it up, then.' Esme put a cup and a coffee pot in front of him.

'The Stone of Scone. It's been stolen.'

'What?'

'Exciting, isn't it?'

Max looked up from his bacon and eggs. 'That's big news for Christmas morning.'

Elliot didn't return his gaze. He turned to the rest of the table and the edge in his voice was unmistakable.

'And I beat the press tycoon to it. What bliss!'

More hostility towards Max Coyle. The house was humming with it. There was a moment's awkwardness, but Dorothy broke it.

'What's the Stone of Scone?' she asked. 'Should I know?'

'The Stone of Destiny.'

'What's that?'

'Good lord!' Elliot threw up his hands in mock horror. 'What do they teach in schools nowadays?'

'Never heard of it.'

'It's the ancient coronation stone of the Scottish kings,' said

Godfrey, behind us. 'Brought from Iona in the Dark Ages to Scone Palace.'

'Till Edward the First removed it,' added Max.

'Till Edward the First stole it,' Ben corrected him quietly.

I caught Andrew's quick smile of approval. Though he looked and sounded like an Englishman, the Scotsman wasn't too far below the surface.

Max, meanwhile, was glaring at Ben.

'Are you Scottish?'

'No.'

'You sound like a nationalist.'

'I'm sorry. I meant to sound like a republican.'

Ben's tone was light but the mockery in his eyes was unmistakable and Max bristled with anger.

'Is nothing sacred to you reds?'

'Well, we're quite fussy about the will of the people. Which brings us neatly back to the Stone of Destiny, doesn't it?'

I thought Max was about to throw a punch, but Esme interrupted the sparring with more questions for Elliot.

'Someone broke into Westminster Abbey? On Christmas Eve?'

'Yes. Whipped it away in the early hours.'

'But why does it matter?' asked Dorothy.

'It's a symbol for the Scots,' said Ishbel. 'Of independence.'

'What a story!' Godfrey turned to Max. 'I suppose the papers will be full of it?'

'If my people are doing what I pay them for.' He turned his attention from Ben to Andrew. 'I'll need to use your phone, if I may.'

'Of course.'

'Is it definitely the nationalists who stole it?' asked Godfrey.

'There was nothing about that in the news,' Eliot said. 'Seems likely though.'

'Good for them,' said Ivy.

The look that passed between her and Ben then was brief but lovely. They really were kindred spirits.

'You approve of stealing from a church on Christmas Day?'

Max's tone was aggressive but if he thought he could intimidate Ivy, he was mistaken.

'I don't see it like that, Mr Coyle. I'm not religious.'

At the sideboard, helping herself to coffee, Sonya laughed.

'Neither is he, honey. Don't worry.' She spoke without turning. 'Max worships nothing but money and power. He's using fake outrage to win an argument. It's a gutter press trick.'

I waited for an outburst from Max, but it didn't come. His eyes were cold and his smile dangerous, but his voice was level.

'If you'll excuse me, I have newspapers to run.'

He threw down his napkin and walked out. I felt rather than heard the collective sigh of relief as the door closed behind him.

'Peace and goodwill to all men,' remarked Elliot archly.

The mood in the room had taken a bit of a dip but whatever Esme's private thoughts, as a hostess, she was equal to it.

'Have we all had enough to eat?' She looked round the table. 'There'll be soup and sandwiches at about two and Christmas dinner at eight. Those so inclined may do a stint in the kitchen, but there is no obligation. Put your feet up or wade through the snow outside. There are wellingtons and coats in the boot room. Whatever you like, darlings. Just make yourselves at home.'

Equanimity was restored and the breakfast party broke up happily enough.

'What are your plans for the morning?' I asked Ivy as we got to our feet. I saw her glance around the room and knew who she was looking for but he had already gone out. 'I heard him say something to Andrew about chopping wood,' I said quietly.

'Behave.'

'Just keeping you informed.'

'Thank you.'

'You're welcome. So what about you?'

'I'll give a hand in the kitchen. Then a quick walk, I think. Then the library.'

'I thought you'd be straight to the books,' I teased her. 'Very restrained.'

'Not at all.' She grinned. 'Just saving the best for last.'

8

Ben Newman had volunteered to chop wood for kindling because he had never felt more inclined to swing an axe. In the bitter cold, as wood chips joined the snow in the air around him, he asked himself, for about the hundredth time, why the hell he had accepted the invitation to Black Gairy? Yes, it was beautiful and yes, Esme and Andrew were welcoming hosts, but still he felt like a square peg in a round hole.

It wasn't his background that set him apart. There were all kinds of people with all kinds of pasts here, he knew that. Well-intentioned people on the whole, but so ignorant of how the system works, its built-in divisions and ruthlessly preserved inequalities. Happy with the status quo or resigned to its permanence. Wilfully unaware and resistant to change.

Looking at the faces around the breakfast table, he was confronted by the enormity of the task ahead, the long road to social justice. He had been fighting for it most of his life, in and out of political parties that inevitably disappointed him, in meetings in smoky rooms, on marches, in protests and on battlefields. For a while, after the Labour landslide in '45, it seemed within reach, but the vested interests of centuries aren't beaten so easily. The same men in the same institutions were still calling the shots. It wasn't easy to keep going, to keep the faith. In a world that celebrated and rewarded Max Coyle, what hope was there?

Ben brought the axe down on the split log before him and watched it splinter. It was an invigorating, grimly satisfying task, just what he needed to see off his dejection. By the time he had worked his way through the wood pile, he felt better. For every Max Coyle there's a Nye Bevan, he reminded himself. We fight the same battles over and over. They don't call it 'the struggle' for nothing. His thoughts turned to his new play and its unambiguous message and he smiled to himself. That was something he could do. His contribution.

As often happened these days, Ivy came into his mind. He remembered the smile she gave him across the table earlier, during the talk about the Stone of Destiny, the way it made him feel. Ivy, in her red sweater, her bright eyes meeting his. He didn't include her in his assessment of the others. She was different. She had resistance in her veins. The first time they spoke, he knew they were made of the same stuff, that they were a fit.

Lowering the axe, he leant on it and raised his face to the heavy, white sky. He felt the snowflakes land cold on his skin and melt away and his heart swelled with sudden joy. The answer to his question, of course, was that he was here because of Ivy Earnshaw. That was no secret, even to her. He had told her too soon and had kicked himself for it but it didn't change anything. There would be another chance, he had seen enough in her eyes to be sure of that. Next time he would do better. He was used to fighting for what he wanted and he had never wanted anything more than he wanted Ivy Earnshaw.

9

IVY

When I thought about spending Christmas at Black Gairy, I had a few flights of fancy, but never for a minute did I imagine Sonya Stirling, with a pinny over her couture dress, up to her elbows in washing up water, scrubbing away at a porridge pan. Then again, the whole scene in the kitchen looked like something from one of her screwball comedies, with Elliot wafting a tea towel ineffectually and Esme on a short set of steps, handing pots down from a high cupboard to Holly and Ishbel waiting below, like a disaster waiting to happen.

'Heroic efforts at the sink,' Esme called from on high, 'but we have a machine for that now. Just to your right, Sonya. It's a miracle.'

'It might be.' Sonya didn't cease her efforts. 'But it's full.'

'You can wait for a second load. Save your manicure.'

'I'm fine. This isn't the first oatmeal pan I've dealt with. Nearly done now.'

I looked around for something to do. At the huge range, Jean MacRae was tending to steaming pans, assisted by a freckle-faced young woman wearing overalls and boots like a land army girl, her hair held back with a scarf and not a trace of make-up. She caught my eye and smiled.

'You're Ivy, aren't you? I'm Fiona.'

'Good to meet you. How can I help?'

'Take your pick. There's veggie peeling, sandwich making, drying the dishes. And somebody needs to organise the fridge and make more room.'

The cavernous kitchen was a mixture of original features and the latest modern comforts. It had a deep Belfast sink, beautiful old copper pans hanging from hooks, gleaming, up-to-date, chrome gadgets on the worktops, the aforesaid dishwasher and an enormous American double-door Frigidaire on the back wall.

'Did you say organise?' Holly called from across the room. 'Then Ivy's your girl.'

She's right. Can't deny it. I chose the fridge and spent the next half hour happily filing the food. Don't laugh. I resisted the temptation to do it alphabetically!

Just as I finished, the back door opened with a gust of cold air, and Ben came in carrying a basket of neatly chopped kindling. He was muffled up in a scarf and gloves, his normally pale face pink with cold. There was snow in his hair. When he looked across at me, I had to remind myself to breathe.

'Sweet Jesus, were you born in a barn?' Elliot shivered theatrically. 'Close the door!'

Ben did as he was told.

'Where do you want this?' he asked Esme.

'In the scullery for now, my dear. Thank you.'

I was overwhelmed by the need to be alone. As soon as Ben was out of sight, I escaped and ran upstairs to my room. It was snowing again, thick flakes obscuring the view from the window.

'Coward,' said the voice in my head. 'Bloody coward.'

I reached for my handbag and took out the photo I've carried in my purse for over ten years. Sam and me on our wedding day. June the 5th 1939, when Ivy Collins became Ivy Earnshaw. I had just turned twenty and looked even younger, little more than a child in my white lace dress and veil. There I am, staring up at Sam like all my wishes have come true. He's smiling into the camera, his cheeky grin. The lock of sandy hair I smoothed back so many times is falling over his forehead. You can't see his freckles in the photo. He was twenty-two. A year later, he was dead.

Holly's Christmas present to me was on the bedside table. I leafed through it until I found the poem I was looking for.

Ae fond kiss, and then we sever
Ae fareweel alas, forever.

I had a little cry. For me, but for Sam too, for everything he was robbed of. I hadn't grieved for him like this for years. Time does its thing, it has to or we'd all be destroyed by loss. We don't 'get over it' but we learn to live with it. I thought I had, but it was all stirred up again because Ben Newman came knocking on a closed door and I was too scared to open it.

After a bit, I pulled myself together and went downstairs. I borrowed a pair of wellies and a waxed coat from the boot room by the front door and went out into the snow. It was falling so heavily I couldn't see the trees beyond the lawn and even in the shelter of the porch, the freezing air stung like little needles. I found a pair of gloves in one of the coat pockets.

They were too big, but they were warm and I was glad of

them. Someone had cleared the steps and made a narrow path around the house. Everything else was buried in white, still and unnaturally quiet.

I turned right and walked past the drawing room windows. Max Coyle was in there, sitting on his own, drinking scotch and reading a sheaf of papers. It looked like work. Christmas Day and still he couldn't loosen his grip. Why on earth would a woman like Sonya Stirling marry a man with no joy in him? I didn't get it.

Walking round the side of the house, I passed the French windows and there was Godfrey in his chair, deep in conversation with Andrew.

The path continued round to the back door and the kitchen, but on my left, the ground rose gently to a small summer house in the shelter of a clump of trees. Leading from the terrace to its door, a line of deep footprints scarred the otherwise untouched snow. Just one set, in one direction.

Whoever had trudged up there hadn't come back the same way. Or was still inside. A quick calculation told me who it was likely to be and I hesitated. If Dorothy wanted to be alone, I didn't want to intrude. But she hadn't looked happy at breakfast and there was something about Dorothy Drake that made me want to help her if I could. I turned off the path and followed her tracks, the snow almost over my boots and thick in the air all around me.

The summer house was a wooden octagon with a conical roof and windows set in seven walls with an arched doorway in the eighth. The bare stems of climbing plants, which would be profuse in the summer, wound all over it. It was easy to imagine Bilbo Baggins living there, but today it held Dorothy, sitting on an old wooden bench, swathed in a fur coat but still shivering. And crying. She looked up as I entered, her pretty face stained with tears, her make-up ruined.

'Oh, love,' I said as I closed the door behind me. 'What's all this?'

'Nothing.' She wiped away her tears but they kept coming. 'I'm all right.'

'Well, you aren't, are you?'

She put her face in her hands. I sat and put my arms around her as her body heaved with sobs. I didn't say anything. I just held her till she calmed down, which took a while. Eventually she was still and we sat together in silence for a few minutes, watching the snow falling outside the seven windows. How strange to be here, I thought. In this lonely place, with a young woman I barely know. On Christmas Day. At home in Morecambe it would be noisy, jolly mayhem, with the whole family packed into Mum's front room, watching my sisters' kids opening their presents, pulling crackers, laughing and joking and, at some point arguing, but getting over it by the time we all sat down to dinner at the familiar table. A wave of homesickness washed over me, a longing for my comfort zone, for the people I love, who love me.

'Thank you.' Dorothy's voice brought me back to the summer house. 'I'm sorry.' Her make-up was nearly all wiped away and she looked so young in her glamorous furs, like a little girl playing dress-up in her mum's clothes.

'No need to apologise,' I told her. 'I'm sorry you're upset. Do you want to talk about it? You don't have to, but, if you want to...'

She nodded assent but didn't start talking. I waited whilst

she twisted her handkerchief in her hands and searched for the courage to speak.

'It's just – I'm not encouraging him. I'm not.' The floodgates opened. 'But Sonya hates me. And Esme. I see you all looking and judging and it's not fair. It isn't me. It's him. He won't leave me alone.'

'You mean Max, of course?'

'He says he can make me a huge star. Or he can ruin me. He says it's up to me.'

I stared at her, horrified. I knew the man was a snake. That's why I was here with Holly in the first place. Of course he would use his power to get what he wanted. I wasn't shocked to have it confirmed, but to be up close, to see and hear it was a different thing altogether. It knocked me for six.

'He threatened you?'

'He'll do it too. Do you remember Vivienne Dean? She was on the way to being a huge star till Coyle's papers hounded her, lied about her, humiliated her. He killed her career because she wouldn't sleep with him.' Dorothy's face was wretched, her eyes full of fear. 'I don't know what to do!'

'You can't give in to him, Dorothy.'

'Easy for you to say.'

She was right. Even though every part of me was screaming, 'Don't let him win', it wasn't up to me.

'I'm not presuming to know how you feel,' I told her, 'but you aren't alone now. I'll help you. Others will help you.'

'He wants to come to my room tonight.'

I actually shuddered. I couldn't help myself. It was repulsive.

'Do you want us to confront him?'

'No! No, please.' She was shaking with panic. 'Don't let him know I told you. Please!'

'It's all right. Don't worry. He won't find out. I promise.' I took hold of her hands, cupped them in mine. She was freezing. 'What can I do to help you?'

She shook her head helplessly. 'I think he'll come to my door, whatever I say.'

'Does it have a lock?'

'Yes.' She started to cry again. 'I don't want him near me.'

'Then we'll make sure he isn't.'

'He'll destroy me.'

I wanted to march down to the house and hit Max Coyle with something heavy. I wanted to see fear in his face, give him a taste of his own medicine. How many times had he done this? How many lives had been at his mercy?

'Listen,' I said, 'let's deal with one thing at a time. Ben's room is on the top floor with yours, isn't it?'

'Yes. And Elliot's and Ishbel's.'

'Let's keep it on a need-to-know basis. You lock your door and Ben will keep an eye on it. You'll be safe. That's the first step. Then we'll think about his threats and how to put a spoke in his wheel. He's a powerful man but we know people with influence too. Like I said, you aren't alone.'

She pulled her hands free and threw her arms around me, still crying but I think more with relief than desperation now.

'Thank you, Ivy,' she said into my shoulder. 'Elliot was right about you.'

'Elliot?'

'He said you were indomitable.'

'Did he now?' I was surprised and flattered. Elliot is sparing in his compliments at the best of times. 'Well, I'd better live up to his expectations then. Come on. Let's show Max Coyle who's boss, shall we?'

*

I knew Ben would be happy to help but it was awkward approaching him with things as they were between us. I owed him a response to what he said last night, I knew that, and I'd deal with it, I would. But just now, we had something else to talk about, so I took a deep breath and went to look for him.

He was in the library. I'd saved a visit there like you save an unopened present or the favourite bit of food on your plate. It was going to be my treat to myself. There aren't many things I love more than wooden shelves of old books floor to ceiling and a comfy chair by the fire. Of course, it was everything I'd imagined. A little bit of paradise. But savouring it had to wait. Ben was alone in there and it was the perfect opportunity to enlist him to the cause.

'Don't worry,' he said when I'd finished my tale. 'Tell Dorothy to lock her door and if Coyle comes anywhere near, I'll take him on with pleasure.'

'Thank you.'

'I told you he was a bastard. Some lives do more than their share of damage but he's head and shoulders above the competition.'

His face and voice were grim and I was too nosey to keep silent.

'What did he do to you, Ben?'

'To me individually? Nothing.'

'So what...?'

He didn't answer.

'Ben?'

He let his breath out slowly before he spoke.

'You know I'm Jewish?'

'Yes.'

'A non-conforming Jew, an atheist, but still a Jew. And Coyle supported the Nazis. His papers amplified them, raised them at first, till it became unpopular to say so. Max Coyle is a fascist and I take that personally.'

I was scared to ask, but I had to.

'Did you lose people? In the camps?'

He shook his head.

'We've been here for generations. We have no family ties in Europe now.'

'There are no words,' I said awkwardly.

'No.' He looked out of the window, but I could tell he wasn't seeing the view. When he carried on, it was as if he was talking to himself. 'I was a teenager when Mosley and the BUF marched on the East End. Coyle's papers were top of the pile that applauded them.'

'I remember.'

I recalled my mum and dad in the newsagents, looking at the headlines in disgust.

'When I was with the International Brigade in Spain, Coyle was a cheerleader for Franco. And he was a big fan of Herr Hitler. His headlines only changed when war became inevitable.'

'I didn't know you fought in Spain. That was a hard fight to lose.'

'It was devastating. We believed in the cause, heart and soul. Someone had to stand against the fascists.' There was grim determination in his face.

'And three years later, you did it again.'

'The politicians were warned that Spain was just the beginning, but they sat on their hands. Hitler and Mussolini were empowered and we were back fighting the same evil.'

Strange to think he was only a few years on from combat, from daily danger and slaughter. I thought of what he must have witnessed, what terrors must haunt his dreams.

'They were defeated in the end,' I said.

'For now.'

I stared at him in horror. 'You think it could happen again?'

'With men like Coyle in power, of course it could. If we aren't vigilant.'

His face was taut with anger, but I watched it soften as he looked at me. What I saw in his eyes made my heart skip a beat. I held my nerve and took a deep breath.

'What you said last night – about why you came here.'

'It wasn't a surprise, was it?'

'No. But...'

I trailed off. It was no good. I couldn't tell him I was too scared to be happy.

'I knew the first time I met you,' he said.

It was my cue to say so did I, but the words wouldn't come. Pathetic, Ivy. He must think I'm a waste of time. I half expected him to walk away. But instead he just smiled.

'It's all right,' he said quietly. 'I'll be here when you're ready.'

10

Dorothy Drake stood in the falling snow outside the drawing room windows, looking in through the leaded panes of glass. She was as still as a statue, as pale as marble. Only her eyes burned as she watched Max Coyle rise from his chair to pour himself another whisky. He didn't look out, didn't see her. Settling himself again, he went back to his papers. Dorothy didn't move. The snow was thick on her blonde hair and the dark fur of her coat but she was oblivious to the cold, conscious only of the rage shooting through her body, the suppressed fury of years breaking free.

How many men had she smiled at through her disgust, men old enough to be her father, her grandfather? Not yet out of her teens and she had lost count of the leering faces and reaching hands. All for one thing, to be a star, to live the dream. Well, she had it now. She had earned it. And no one was going to take it away. No one.

Dorothy unclenched her freezing hands. There were red semicircles on her palms where her nails had dug into them. Standing in the swirling snow, she closed her eyes and made a solemn vow. No more. Never again. And if Max Coyle came for her, he would be stopped. Whatever it took.

11

HOLLY

It was understood that we would all make our best sartorial effort for Christmas dinner. I selected my favourite Pierre Balmain gown in black and olive silk, which covered all the right places and pinched and tucked to perfection. My hair was behaving itself for once, I had peridots in old gold at my ears and throat and, looking in the mirror, I decided that I was pleasantly pleased with the overall result.

'Lovely.' Ivy stood in the bathroom doorway.

'Thank you, darling. And you.'

Her frock had a shawl collar and a waist bow, and was a deep rose pink that suited her dark colouring perfectly. She had opals in her ears and a row of tiny silk roses tucked into her curls at each side.

'You've never looked better,' I told her. 'Shall we face the fray?'

There it was again, that frisson of foreboding. We were about to have a delicious dinner in a beautiful house, as guests of a dear friend and her charming husband. It was Christmas, the season of goodwill. And yet, I felt the need to hold myself in readiness.

Ivy had told me about her meeting with Dorothy in the summer house and the plan for Ben to keep an eye on her door later tonight. A predatory man is not unusual or even unexpected in our world, but Max Coyle is a particularly unpleasant example. *Is he doing the same to Esme?* was my first thought. *Surely not under her own roof with her husband here?* It seemed a lot of people had an issue with him and he seemed to relish it. As well as poor Dorothy and Esme, Sonya was clearly livid with him, and Elliot couldn't conceal his dislike.

I didn't know if I was uneasy or excited. What was I expecting to happen? I couldn't say exactly. Just that something was simmering at Black Gairy. And still the snow fell, deeper and deeper, and we must be cut off soon.

'Penny for 'em.' Ivy was holding the door, waiting to go downstairs. She smiled when I looked up. 'You were miles away for a minute.'

'Sorry, darling.'

'I wondered if you were missing Vincent?'

It was a shock to realise I hadn't given him a thought for days. Eighteen months together and some lovely times but no, I wasn't missing him at all. He never took root, bless him. So few do.

'You're sweet, but no. My thoughts are Vincent-free. Awful of me, isn't it?'

'New pastures, then.'

'I suppose so.'

'The hurly burly of the chaise longue.'

'What?'

'It's what Mrs Campbell said about her single life.'

'Ah yes. Mrs Pat. I worked with her between the wars. An Ibsen play. Awful production. But she was a force of nature. I don't mind being compared to her at all.'

'There's more to that quote. About marriage. The deep, deep peace of the double bed.'

'That sounds nice.'

'My mum laughed her head off when she read it. Said Mrs Patrick Campbell had obviously never heard my dad snoring!'

'Ah well, chaise longue it is then. Shall we make a move?'

*

In the drawing room, champagne corks were popping and there was a party atmosphere that made my earlier dread seem melodramatic and a little foolish. Godfrey's jacket was a festive claret red and he wore tasselled slippers to match. Elliot and Ben were in black tie and Andrew was resplendent in formal Highland dress – green and blue tartan kilt, short velvet jacket, white stockings and black buckle brogues.

'Is that sharp?' Dorothy pointed to the horn handle of the *sgian dubh* tucked into the rolled top of his right sock.

'Yes, it has an edge. But the sheath keeps it safe.' Andrew reached down and took it out. The short blade was held in a tooled leather case.

'It looks old.'

'It's a good age. Been in the family for generations.'

'And that must be the Fergusson tartan?'

'There are a few, actually.' Andrew replaced the dagger. 'But we have always worn this one.'

'Ishbel too,' I said. She was in deep blue velvet with a wide plaid sash over one shoulder. 'You look very lovely.'

'Yes, indeed. Jack is a lucky man!'

68

Elliot's face was all innocence but I caught the faint sting in his voice. Ishbel was clearly hiding something about her absent boyfriend. When I asked about him, she answered calmly enough, but I know a rehearsed performance when I see one. Elliot must have noticed it too and it's in his nature to stir troubled waters, not sooth them. I gave him a warning look but he showed no sign of being chastened. Ishbel's smile didn't waver but a flush crept up her neck and mottled her pale cheeks. As usual, Esme came to the rescue.

'Everyone looks utterly splendid!'

She started handing out glasses of champagne. Her frock was close-fitting and low-backed in a shimmering silver that moved like liquid. Diamonds flashed at her throat and in her ears. She looked extraordinarily beautiful and Andrew had the air of a man who couldn't believe his good fortune.

'Just Sonya and Max to come, then we can sit down to dinner. Esme chattered on as Ishbel recovered her composure. 'The wonderful MacRaes are going to wait on us tonight so we can do the thing properly. Honestly, they deserve medals. Morag Murray was going to come up from the village to help but there's too much snow, so she stayed at home and they've lost a pair of hands. But Jean is unflappable.'

Elliot's amusement gave way to puzzlement but Sonya and Max arrived and diverted his attention. The venom in his eyes as they turned on Max shocked me. Not just his usual acidity but something deeper and uglier. He moved away and helped himself to another glass of wine, but I felt something dark had entered the room. I almost shivered.

'Are you all right?'

Ivy was at my elbow, with Ben at hers.

'Absolutely,' I assured them. I lowered my voice. 'But what on earth has Max come as?'

'Behave.'

'I'm sorry, darling, but really.'

Max Coyle was also in a kilt and all the trimmings. His shirt had a ruffled lace jabot, his kilt pin and sporran were embellished with gem stones, as was the long silver handle of the sgian dubh in his sock, and the tartan was a garish check in yellow and black. It was all wrong. Too much. Whilst Andrew seemed born to the clothes, Max looked like something out of central casting.

Sonya made her way to her favourite spot by the fireplace but Max maintained his stance in the doorway, as if awaiting comment, and as no one else seemed inclined, I stepped up to the plate.

'I didn't know you wore Highland dress, Max. How wonderful! What's the tartan?'

'This is the Coyle. Specially commissioned for today. A slice of Scottish heritage, bought and paid for.'

I had walked right into it and given him the opportunity to flaunt his wealth, insult his hosts and belittle Scots culture all in the same breath. Well done, Elspeth.

In the uncomfortable silence that followed, Max scanned the room until he found Dorothy, sitting on the arm of a sofa, her dress and lips scarlet, her blonde curls piled high on her head. She was a study in contrived nonchalance, but her eyes sought out Ivy and Ben and with a nod to me they casually took up their posts on either side of her. Like sentinels, bless them.

'Any more news on the Stone, Max?' asked Godfrey.

'They've closed the border between England and Scotland and put up roadblocks.'

'Closed the border?' Ivy whistled.

'A policeman spotted what he thought was a courting couple in a Ford Anglia outside the Abbey. At three in the morning. Idiot waved them off without a second thought. Probably had the Stone in the boot.'

'It must weigh a tonne,' said Ben. 'I don't hold out much hope for the car's suspension!'

'The bobby said they had Scottish accents. And dressed like students.' Max looked across at Ishbel. 'Might be one of your lot at Glasgow. You might know them.'

'There are about five thousand of us,' Ishbel replied shortly. 'I'm not on speaking terms with all of them.'

'But the place is a hotbed of Nationalism, isn't it?'

'Not to my knowledge.'

'Well, the Rector's one of them.'

'John MacCormick? He's for devolution not independence.'

'Same thing.'

'It really isn't.'

'Well, whoever did it will be caught, and soon.' Max seemed surprised and none too pleased to be contradicted. His tone was dismissive. 'I've got a couple of my best bloodhounds on it. We'll get it back.'

'Max thinks this is the scoop that will get him into the Lords.' Sonya was fitting a cigarette into her holder as she spoke for the first time. She was wearing jade silk brocade, her plentiful hair swept off her face in a heavy French twist. When she raised her head and surveyed the room, her eyes gleamed as green as the emeralds in her ears. 'He thinks it's well overdue. Twenty-five years since he got his knighthood for services rendered to the Tory Party. Time to move up, isn't it, darling?'

I must say, I was a little cross with her. I had no expectations of Max's behaviour, but Sonya, whatever her personal circumstances, ought to have known better than to embarrass her hosts. It was obvious, however, that she had warmed up with a few pre-dinner drinks before joining us for champagne and as she wasn't exactly inhibited when she was sober, there was nothing holding her back now she was lubricated. I saw Esme take a step forward, but before she could speak, Sonya started up again.

'You know how he got to be Sir Max, don't you? He invented a scandal. The Fedorov Conspiracy. Remember that? His papers were full of it for weeks. Stole the '24 election from Labour. Only it was pure fiction, wasn't it, darling? A pack of lies. You made it up. Every word.'

Max shrugged his shoulders.

'That's old news, Sonya. Try harder.'

'Fedorov?' asked Dorothy.

'Before your time, darling.' Elliot patted her arm. 'A group of young communists were accused of being Russian agents infiltrating the Labour Party. We were all terrified of the reds in those days. Rather like America now.'

'There were riots,' Ishbel added. 'Someone was killed.'

'Harry Parker,' said Ben.

I remembered the front pages as if it was yesterday. The photographs. The young faces in a row, names underneath, like wanted posters. Not one of them over twenty. And Harry Parker in the middle, alive and well and looking into a future that never happened.

'Max set the mob on them,' Sonya pushed on. 'But he got his knighthood. Hey ho.'

She stopped and there was an apprehensive silence. Was there more to come? But it was Max who spoke next.

'I apologise for my wife. She's drunk.'

'Not quite,' Sonya bit back. 'Not yet.' And then she laughed and I could read her thoughts. She was laughing at herself, at the situation and the absurdity of her anger. It was human and charming and it won all of us over, in spite of the scene she had just caused. She slugged back the last of her champagne and with mischief in her eyes, she faced the room.

'Fasten your seat belts—'

Her Bette Davis impression was faultless and *All About Eve* had been the film of the year. We all knew the rest and there was a general chorus.

'It's going to be a bumpy night!'

After our laughter, Sonya spread her arms and gave us a dazzling smile.

'I apologise for myself. The drama is over. Is it dinner time now? I'm starving.'

And so we all trooped into the dining room and took our places at the table. I didn't know about anyone else, but I felt positively skittish with champagne and relief. I was seated between Godfrey and Esme and sensed the tension in them both. We were all drinking too much, trying too hard. Max and Sonya found places as far apart as possible, eating heartily and seemingly unaware of the undercurrents that flowed around them. It was unfair of me, I know, but I blamed Max's malign presence, even though it was Sonya's behaviour that had wrecked the mood. Who wouldn't behave badly, married to him?

Thankfully, as the wine flowed and the delicious food kept coming, the festive atmosphere was restored. Esme and I talked about our happy place – the theatre. We swapped stories, some old, some new, and we laughed like drains.

'Remember when the door in the set was stuck, just wouldn't open, and Johnny had to exit through the fireplace?'

'And the time I was directed to sit at the table, sewing, and I managed to stitch through the fabric and the tablecloth and my costume, so I was fixed to the set and couldn't exit at all till the interval!'

I met Donald MacRae for the first time as he was helping Jean and Fiona serve the meal. He was a short, stocky man with thick red hair and a close beard of the same colour. As he placed platter after platter in front of us, he smiled but didn't speak until I opened a conversation.

'When will you have your Christmas dinner, Mr MacRae?'

'We'll sit down later, nae bother. That's fine by us. We don't make the same fuss of Christmas as the English.'

His accent was strong but he was easier to understand than his wife. I didn't need Esme to translate this time.

'Of course. Your holiday is Hogmanay.'

'Aye. We have a dram or two then.'

Ivy said, 'I read somewhere that Christmas was illegal in Scotland at one time.'

She was on the other side of Godfrey, next to Ben. Darling

Ivy has always read something somewhere. The things she knows are extraordinary.

'Aye, that's right. Not so long since.'

'I had no idea!' Esme called to Andrew further down the table. 'You're failing in my Scottish education.'

'I am a poor teacher.' Andrew smiled at her.

'I forgive you.'

I checked Max out of the corner of my eye. He was refilling his glass and if he was disappointed by this show of affection, he didn't show it.

'Well, thank you for indulging us,' I said to Donald. 'It's all wonderful.'

'You're welcome.'

He nodded and departed.

'Donald is a man of few words,' said Esme. 'But he's one of the best. He was a foreman in the shipyard. A loyal union man. Didn't let the bosses get away with anything, Andrew says.'

'A Clydeside Red.' Godfrey was a bit tipsy, which was unusual for him but understandable in the circumstances. 'Salt of the earth.'

'Seriously, darling,' I laughed. 'What do you know about Glaswegian trade unions?'

'For your information, young Elspeth, I narrated a documentary about the Battle of George Square when Churchill sent in the troops to break the strike. Next question.'

'I stand corrected.'

'We owe a debt of gratitude.' He raised his glass. 'To those who fight and die for progress.'

'I never had you down as a radical, Godfrey.'

75

'I'm not. But better people are, and the debt must be acknowledged. "Attention must be paid."'

He was drunker than I thought. I joined him in his toast and raised an eyebrow at Esme, who gave him a fond smile.

The meal continued happily. The flaming Christmas pudding was brought in and there was much hilarity looking for the sixpence until Dorothy found it in her portion and was duly congratulated.

I didn't notice Max leaving the room but suddenly the door to the hall opened and he came back in, a look of profound irritation on his face.

'The phone line is dead. No calls in or out.'

'I'm surprised it took this long.' Andrew was unperturbed. 'I don't expect it will be fixed in a hurry either in this snow.'

'But I can't be out of touch with my people. That's out of the question.'

'I'm afraid it is what it is. You could try the village post office tomorrow, if the roads are passable. But I wouldn't hold my breath.'

'Ridiculous.' Max threw himself into his chair with a face like thunder.

'It might do you good to switch off for a day or two. The world will keep turning without you.'

'Ah,' Sonya smiled. 'But he won't be dictating the speed and direction. Can't have that, can we?'

Esme was on her marks this time. She sprang up like a jack-in-the-box and waved towards the drawing room.

'We need some music. It's that time. Elliot, will you give us a song?'

'Oh yes,' I chimed in, receiving a grateful smile from Esme. 'Time to sing for your supper, darling. I'd love to hear something.'

He was chivvied to the grand piano, not actually reluctant but playing a little hard to get, as is the tradition. Once there, of course, all that fell away and he did what he does best, his elegant hands on the keys, his lazy vocals, his songs witty, arch and sometimes sweetly touching. Then he summoned Esme to his side and they sang a duet before she gave us a song on her own. For the next hour or two we entertained each other, as actors do. If we can't give party pieces, who can?

The mood in the room mellowed further as more bottles were opened and emptied. Ivy and Ben were squeezed onto a sofa with Dorothy and seemed happy to be squashed together. Andrew was sitting between his wife and daughter, Sonya and Godfrey on either side of the fire and Max was in the chair next to mine, just behind the piano. Even he seemed to relax as the festivities continued. For the first time, I felt he was fully present, his attention not dispersed. As much as it ever was, I think, his guard was down. It made a difference. With his hard edges softened, I imagined I caught a glimpse of the man he might have been in a different life. No one is all bad, surely?

We finished the night with some carols and everyone joined in. It was lovely. The snowy landscape outside, the lights within, the voices raised in song and the music floating through the beautiful house. There is something wonderful about Christmas, isn't there? Even for those of us with no religion, it's a time to believe in the best of us, which is love, of course, selfless and generous love. We aim for it, we often fail, but for a few days at the end of each year, we acknowledge its power.

'Merry Christmas,' we wished each other as we went up to bed. I may be hopelessly naïve but I believe we all meant it. In that moment, if not later.

12

Esme Arden was alone in the drawing room, the last to go upstairs. She had switched off the lamps and all the fairy lights, except the strings in the window, reflecting in the dark panes like rows of Tinkerbells. Looking past them to the white world outside, she thrust her shaking hands deep into her trouser pockets and tried without success to steady her breathing. She was horribly afraid.

In the dark glass, her reflection stared back at her, pale and wide-eyed, like a judgement. How had she let it get to this? The place she had made for herself here was everything she wanted. She had lived a varied existence and known her share of men, but she had never dreamed that she would find a love like this, a life like this. And now someone was threatening it. Silently she swore an oath to the face in the window. She would do anything to keep it. Anything at all.

'Are you coming up, darling?'

Andrew appeared in the doorway. At the sight of him, an instinct stronger than fear flooded her veins. She threw her arms around him.

'It will be all right, my love,' she told him.

She would make sure of that. For his sake, she would destroy anything in her path and salt the earth behind her.

13

IVY

I woke up as the dawn light was creeping into my room. We'd been late to bed so I hadn't slept long but I felt wide awake so I jumped out of bed and quickly washed and dressed. There was no sound from Holly's room. I went downstairs into the kitchen, in search of a cup of tea. We'd agreed there'd be no formal breakfast this morning, after the merrymaking last night, and that we'd just help ourselves to what we could find. The MacRaes could have a well-earned rest and anyone who wanted to could sleep till lunch.

I drank my tea at the big kitchen table, enjoying the quiet of the sleeping house. I was tossing up whether to have a morning in the library or go for a walk. The call of the books was strong but I decided I felt too energised to stay indoors and a tramp through the snow, maybe to the loch, would be a bit of an adventure. I grabbed the boots and coat I'd worn the day before and let myself out of the front door.

A narrow path had been cleared between the house and the lodge and I made my way down it, towards the gates and the waters of Loch Trool, just visible beyond the trees. It was freezing. I reached for the gloves in the pocket where I'd left them the day before and was disappointed to find them gone.

Should have checked before I set out. I strode on, the frosty air stinging my face and misting before me.

The lodge came into sight round a bend in the drive and I saw Donald MacRae was out and about early too. I waved but he didn't see me. Spade in hand, he disappeared into what looked like a tool shed nestled in the trees by the high estate wall. Up at dawn to clear the snow – he was certainly a grafter. Hopefully he would be on his way in to a comfy chair and a hot brew now.

The wrought-iron gates were standing open. I hadn't really noticed them from the car but it was different on foot. They were tall and wide and beautiful, an intricate design of leaves and flowers on a heavy metal frame, with a huge letter 'F' ornately forged at the centre of each gate. Andrew's grandfather had staked his claim here and no messing.

Once through them, I crossed a patch of rocky grassland to the loch, stretched before me in all its glory, silvered by the winter light, winding through the valley between high hills cloaked in snow. It was spectacular. For a long moment I stood still, just breathing it in.

'You're up early.'

It was Andrew, making his way down a path that rose from the loch side to some sort of monument on a cairn of rough stones at the top.

'That makes two of us.'

'Walking off a hangover,' he laughed. 'One dram too many last night.'

'It was fun.'

'It was. Are you suffering?'

'No. I seem to have got away with it.'

'Lucky you.'

'What is that up there?' I asked.

'Bruce's Stone.'

'Robert the Bruce?'

'It commemorates the battle of Loch Trool. It was his first victory on the road to independence. You should pop up and have a look, while you're here. The view is wonderful.'

'I will.' I looked out at the loch and mountains again. It was hard to tear your eyes from them. 'You're very lucky to have this place.'

'I know it.'

'Why did your grandfather choose here? I mean, I see the appeal, but there's a lot of Scotland. Why this corner?'

Andrew smiled. He was a good-looking man, full of the charm and ease that goes with a posh upbringing. Normally, I'd be put off by all that, even suspicious of it, but not with Andrew Fergusson. There was a generosity about him that outweighed it all. His face was open, his eyes were kind and I couldn't help but like him.

'My grandfather was what he liked to call a self-made man. As a boy, with no money, his idea of recreation was getting out of the city into the hills, to walk and climb. He particularly loved it here.' He raised a hand and pointed to the tallest peak, rising behind the loch. 'That's the Merrick. There's a rock face up there called Black Gairy. It's quite a challenge, but he scaled it often. He said climbing was like life. You hold on tight, ignore the drop and keep pushing upwards. Hence the name of the house.'

'Sounds like he was quite a force.'

'He was a tough man. Not easy to know. But he built quite an empire. He said Clydeside doesn't suffer fools gladly. It chews them and spits them out. "The men in the shipyards are men of mettle." I can't count the times he told me that.'

Didn't stop him making a fortune on the backs of their labour, I thought. But I didn't say it. Sometimes you have to bite your tongue. And anyway, here I was enjoying the fruits of it too, wasn't I? Glass houses, Ivy.

'Enough family history.' Andrew smiled and gestured towards the house. 'I'm ready for some breakfast, are you?'

'I think I'll go up to the monument first.'

'Enjoy.'

We parted company and I walked up the low hill to get a better look at Bruce's Stone. It was a huge boulder, roughly shaped around the edges and mottled with lichen, sitting on a mound of smaller rocks on a raised outcrop that sat high above the loch. There was an inscription carved into the stone:

'In loyal remembrance of Robert the Bruce, King of Scots, whose victory in this glen over an English force in March 1307, opened the campaign of independence which he brought to a decisive close at Bannockburn on 24th June 1314.'

I turned full circle. The ancient landscape stretched for miles all around me. In the quiet I could imagine the clansmen facing their enemy here, almost catch the battle cries echoing on the rocky slopes. And here we were, 600 years later, with the struggle for independence still ongoing. The Stone of Destiny was the top story on all the news bulletins. Whoever had stolen it had done their job and re-ignited the debate in dramatic fashion. The Bruce would be proud of them. Still fighting the fight.

*

Walking back through the gates, I saw Dorothy coming out of the house and quickened my pace to join her on the drive, keen to know if our plan had been successful.

'It worked perfectly,' she said, with a smile. 'Thanks to Ben. And you.'

With her long-lashed eyes and full red lips, she looked at ease and beautiful in her sable coat, a chocolate brown scarf around her head and neck. A weight seemed to have fallen from her. I was glad to see it but curious about the extent of the transformation. I'd say we won the battle but not the war, not yet.

'Max turned up then?' I asked.

'Oh yes. Three in the morning. Full of whisky. He was furious to find my door locked but I just pretended to be asleep. Then Ben came out of his room and ordered him away.'

'And he went? Just like that?'

'They argued. Till Ben suggested waking Andrew and Esme and that did the trick. Max threatened him, in his usual style. Said Ben would never get another play produced, that he'd find the skeletons in his cupboard and tell the world. Then he stormed off.'

That was worrying. It hadn't occurred to me that there could be any repercussions for Ben but of course Max Coyle would hit back. I felt a pang of guilt.

'I don't think he believes that I was asleep,' Dorothy continued, 'but I don't care. Let him do his worst. We have a story of our own to tell now, don't we?'

'That's right.'

She reached out and took my hand.

'Thank you, Ivy.'

'What did I do? I was fast asleep!'

'You gave me the push I needed to fight back. I've already done something I wouldn't have dreamed of doing before now. It didn't work but I'll try again, given the chance. I'm playing him at his own game now.'

'I don't follow?'

I could see she regretted saying so much. Withdrawing her hand, she adjusted her headscarf, though it didn't need it. Her pretty face had closed off.

'It doesn't matter.'

'I'm glad you feel better,' I said. 'But please tread carefully.'

'Don't worry.'

'He's a nasty piece of work.'

'I know. It's fine. And you were a friend in need. I'll remember that.'

With that, she carried on with her walk, leaving me feeling a bit anxious. I hoped Ben was all right. Had we acted unwisely? It was risky to antagonise a man like Max Coyle. A man with the power to install governments. I remembered him boasting at the dinner table, how it was down to him that Labour's huge majority was nearly wiped out in the election this year. And how, when there was a rerun next year, as he assured us there would be, he'd finish the job and put the Tories back in.

'Papers are like polls,' he said. 'We don't reflect public opinion, we form it.'

His smile of self-satisfaction made my blood boil, all the more so because I knew he was right. He was powerful and vindictive and a very dangerous enemy. We had known that when we took him on, but what choice did we have? Now Dorothy seemed to be throwing caution to the wind and I was worried I'd created a monster.

Inside I looked for Holly, then Ben and was disappointed to find neither of them downstairs so, after a quick breakfast, I went to the library and settled myself in for a morning of quiet bliss. There was a fire in the hearth – someone had been busy – and the snow was falling gently again outside the window.

I browsed the shelves, found a beautiful old copy of *Nicholas Nickleby* and that, as they say, was that. Next thing I knew, the clock on the mantelpiece was striking two and the door opened to admit Holly, a vision in aquamarine.

'No prizes for finding you!'

'Good afternoon.'

'I know. So late. How decadent! Esme sent me to announce lunch.'

'Oh, good, I'm hungry.'

'Me too, darling. I'm ravenous. Must be the Scottish air.'

'You haven't set foot over the doorstep yet,' I laughed.

'That's all you know.' She linked arms as we crossed the hall. 'I was out on the terrace before I joined you – until I nearly broke my neck on a patch of ice under the snow. Outside is dangerous!'

As she was speaking, Ben appeared at the top of the stairs and I felt the same quick lurch of my heart at the sight of him. Holly patted my arm and went on into the dining room and I held back till he joined me by the Christmas tree.

'Happy Boxing Day,' I said.

'What's left of it. Sorry I'm so late.'

'And you still look tired out.'

'I'm all right.'

I wasn't convinced. His face was pale and strained, there was an awkwardness in his manner and the smile he gave me seemed forced. 'Shall we get lunch before it's time for dinner?'

He moved off before I had time to answer and I followed him with a sinking heart. Something was bothering him, that was clear enough. Was it Max's threats? Or impatience with me, despite his fine words? Or maybe it was just a really bad hangover. I decided to give him some room and went to sit with Ishbel and Dorothy at the far end of the table whilst he took his plate to the empty chair next to Godfrey.

There was a full gathering including all three MacRaes, who were in and out with dishes of food. Only Max was missing. As the meal progressed, Esme looked up from a hearty portion of game pie and called over the hubbub of voices to Sonya.

'Max wins the sleeping medal today. Do you think he'll come down at all?'

Sonya paused with her fork in the air.

'Max? Haven't seen him.'

'Isn't he in bed?'

'Not in our room. I slept in lonely splendour last night. I assumed he spent the night elsewhere.'

Everyone knew who her words were aimed at. In the sudden hush, Dorothy's cutlery hit her plate with a loud clatter.

'You assumed wrong,' she said steadily. 'I don't blame you for thinking it. I know what it looked like and I know I should have spoken out earlier. But I also slept alone last night. As I always intended to.'

I was proud of Dorothy and her new-found courage. It seemed to impress Sonya too. She turned and they looked at each other for a long moment. It felt like the whole room was holding its breath.

At last Sonya spoke. 'Things aren't always what they seem.'

'No.'

'No.' She drained her glass and put it down. 'It appears I was mistaken. Will you accept my apology? It's sincerely made.'

'Yes.'

'Thank you. That's very gracious.'

The room exhaled.

That's when Elliot spoke. He was lounging in his chair, legs crossed and coffee cup in hand.

'Can I ask?' He paused just long enough, taking us all in, working his audience. 'I'm just wondering – if Max isn't in his room, or in Dorothy's room, and no one has seen him today, then where exactly is he?'

14

HOLLY

It was a quick task to ascertain that Max wasn't in the house.

'That's a puzzle,' said Esme, a note of concern in her voice.

'He must be out for a walk.' Sonya returned to her lunch, seemingly unconcerned.

'All this time?'

'Maybe he's gone into the village as you suggested last night, Andrew.' Ben was at the window, scanning the grounds as he spoke. 'To the post office.'

'Well, all the cars are still in the garages, so wherever he's gone, it was on foot.'

Fiona appeared in the doorway. 'There's a waterproof missing from the boot room.'

'There we are then.' Sonya finished eating and leaned back in her chair. 'He's gone in search of a phone line.'

'But he's been gone for hours.' Esme wasn't convinced. 'What if he's slipped on the ice and hurt himself? He could be lying out there in the cold.'

Bless her. She obviously loathed the man but she couldn't stop being Esme.

Andrew put an arm around her. 'I'll take the car to the village.'

I couldn't help thinking his concern was more for her than for Max but off he went and, in a few moments, we watched the car disappear down the drive and out of the gates.

'Andrew will find him,' I said, with more confidence than I felt. The unease that I had been pushing away for days was growing stronger by the minute and I knew I wasn't alone. There was an unmistakable tension in the room.

'I'll get some drinks.'

The ever-practical Fiona headed for the kitchen and returned with a tray of steaming mulled wine. Glasses in hand, we drifted into the drawing room, making small talk and waiting to hear the car return.

Elliot turned on the wireless and the theme tune of *Dick Barton* blared out of the set.

'Oh, please turn it off!' Esme's voice was unusually sharp.

Elliot complied with a raise of his eyebrows. Sitting on the arm of my chair, he yawned and looked plaintively at the white world outside.

'Still snowing. Will it ever stop?'

'That might be my fault. I wished for a white Christmas.'

'Do you have much influence with the weather gods?'

'It would seem that I do.'

'Well, tell them enough is enough, would you, dear? I want to get home before Easter.'

'Max may come back with more information, if he found a working phone.' Ivy joined us. She was taking the resolutely positive line and I was grateful for it. 'He's probably in the pub chatting up the barmaid.'

'I wish him luck with that.' Sonya drawled from her seat by

the fire. 'We stopped at the pub on our way here. Mrs Boyle is a woman of few words and she was seventy-three last birthday.'

'Funny,' said Elliot. 'You should go on the stage.'

'I would, if only I had the legs.'

'That didn't stop Holly, did it darling?'

'Not at all. I played Peter Pan three Christmases in a row.'

The banter seemed a little inappropriate under the circumstances, but it was a welcome relief.

'How perfect,' quipped Elliot. 'The actress who wouldn't grow up.'

I had an unworthy retort about believing in fairies but it was never uttered as the door opened to admit Andrew and we all turned to greet him. He was still wrapped up in outdoor clothes, snow melting on his hat and overcoat. His face was solemn.

'The roads are impassable by car. I had to abandon it a mile away.'

'Oh, darling, you must be frozen.'

'I'm fine. I walked into the village but no one has seen anything of Max. The phone lines are down there too so we're pretty much cut off until the weather improves.'

'So where on earth is he?'

'He must have had an accident,' Dorothy said. 'Or he'd be back by now, wherever he went.'

Godfrey looked out of the window.

'It will be dark soon.'

'If he's lying out there injured, he needs to be found.' Andrew took Esme's hand. 'We need a search party. Get everyone who can help, darling, and grab some torches.'

We all rushed off to muster the troops and don coats and boots. Godfrey couldn't join us, of course, so Dorothy volunteered to stay with him whilst the rest of us went out into the bitter cold night, splitting into pairs to search the grounds in the fading twilight.

'You go with Ben,' I said to Ivy. 'I'll take charge of Elliot.'

We were given the slope leading up from the patio to the summer house and the two of us trudged through the deep snow in unusual silence, shining our torches into the shadows. I was feeling an unnerving mixture of expectation and apprehension. My heart jumped at every slight movement, as I strained my ears for the faintest sound, the weakest cry for help. There was nothing, just a frozen crunching beneath our feet and our breath misting pale in the darkness around us. It was horrible.

My imagination was on overdrive. What if he had slipped by the loch, hit his head and drowned? What if he was floating there now in the deep, dark water? Or had a heart attack and was lying dead, covered in the day's snowfall, still and white under the trees?

We reached the summer house and I opened the door, my heart in my mouth, but the beam of my torch swept an empty space and I breathed easier for a few minutes. Elliot walked in and took a seat with a great sigh of relief. It was hard going in the snow and the cold air and he had never been the hearty sort.

'Thank the Lord!' he said with feeling. 'Is that us done now? Can we go back to the fire?'

'He's still missing, you heartless creature. We can't just give up.'

'I was afraid you'd say that.'

From the open doorway, I could see flashes of light among the trees and hear Max's name being called in the distance. He hadn't been found yet and I was reluctant to leave the search. It was real now and serious. I thought of Sonya, out there in the night. What must she be feeling?

'Stiffen the sinews, darling. Come on.'

'Is this revenge for my *Peter Pan* comment?'

'And the rest. Up you get.'

He groaned but did as he was told and we set out again, heading into the woods at the side of the house.

After a few minutes, two beams of light approached and our torches picked out Ivy and Ben. We greeted each other like long-lost travellers, disproportionately grateful, in the strangeness of our situation, for the comfort of human contact.

'Nothing,' said Ivy in response to my unasked question. 'You?'

I shook my head and we fell silent. An owl hooted in the trees, loud and startling, and we all jumped out of our skins and then laughed nervously at our skittishness. I was relieved they were as unnerved as I was. Ivy couldn't keep still, moving from one foot to the other. Ben stood slightly apart, staring away into the distance, lost in thought. I opened my mouth to speak, but before I could, a shout of alarm echoed through the darkness and we looked at each other, wide-eyed.

'What was that?'

'I think it was Andrew,' said Elliot.

Ivy ran towards the source of the shout and, after a split second, we followed her as fast as we could, across the frozen ground towards the loch perimeter wall. We threaded through the trees and arrived in a panting group, our torches picking out an awful tableau that will haunt my dreams for as long as I live.

Andrew was holding Sonya, pulling her back from a shallow ditch by the wall. Donald MacRae knelt by a drift of snow banked up against the old stonework. Behind him, his wife and daughter stood with Ishbel and Esme, pale faces stricken with shock.

Instinctively I reached out for Ivy and she took my arm, holding on tight. In my heart I knew what I was looking at, but the detail registered slowly.

Where the snowfall was thinner, there was a slight movement in the night wind. It was a patch of yellow and black tartan, lifting and falling. Something gleamed in the beam from a torch, reflecting shards of light onto the trees. The handle of an ornate silver dagger, set with yellow gemstones.

'I saw something glint in the dark,' said Esme. 'I didn't know what it was till I got closer—' Her voice wavered and stopped.

Donald leaned down and brushed away the snow to reveal the long blade, buried deep in a pale neck, above the blood-sodden frills of a lace jabot. Sonya sagged in Andrew's arms. Ishbel buried her face in Esme's shoulder. At my side, I heard Ivy gasp with horror.

Lying on his side, the face in profile was a lifeless, waxy grey. Whatever you believe, whatever had made him Max Coyle was gone, leaving this empty shell, abandoned in the cold and the dark and far from home.

My imagination hadn't been dark enough, it seemed. No accident. No drowning. No heart attack. Sometime between the early hours and this grim teatime, someone had murdered Max Coyle, stabbed him in the throat with his own *sgian dubh* and left him dead in a ditch. Looking at the ghastly faces around me, I saw the same thought writ clear on all of them. Christmas had taken a gruesome turn. There was a killer at Black Gairy.

15

Ben Newman bent over the fire in his bedroom, poker in hand, staring into the flames with desperation. He made sure that what was burning in the grate was reduced to ashes before he turned away. The poker dropped into the hearth with a clatter as he sank onto his bed and put his head in his hands.

How had he got through today? And what a nightmare it had been, out there in the snow. He had barely held himself together. What a mess he had made. After waiting so long for Ivy and coming so close to winning her, now he couldn't even look her in the face. She knew there was something wrong. He had seen the questions in her eyes. She would voice them soon and what the hell could he say?

He wasn't sorry that Max Coyle was dead. He couldn't pretend that he was. But he had ruined everything. Why did he do it? And what was he going to do now?

16

Dorothy Drake stared into the cheval mirror in the corner of her room, studying her reflection, surprised that she looked the same when she felt so different. It was like the empty space she had carried around for years had been filled and smoothed over. For the first time in her life, she felt solid at the core. How had it happened? Where had it come from? She laughed to herself and watched her face in the oval glass light up with this new happiness. Now she saw the change. Something in her eyes, in the set of her chin. It reminded her of Sonya Stirling, of Dame Elspeth and Ivy. An ease that was new to her. An unfamiliar strength.

Leaving the mirror, she took an envelope from her bedside table drawer and shook out the contents onto her bedspread. Two days since she ran upstairs with it burning a hole in her coat pocket, only two days since her act of rebellion, of retaliation, which had surprised and heartened her. Now this discovery made it irrelevant. Well, for her at least. There was someone else who would be relieved to know that their ordeal was over, that the source of their fear was in safe hands. She was glad she could help them, glad she had done what she had done. No shame. No regret. Max Coyle, alive or dead, didn't deserve either.

17

IVY

'It doesn't feel real, does it?'

Holly shook her head and we stared at each other in silence, trying to process what had happened: the search in the dark, the shocking discovery and the awful sight of Max's body.

I was sitting on the chaise in Holly's bedroom, my arms wrapped around a tapestry cushion, clasping it to my body for protection or comfort, for the reassurance of something solid. I'll not pretend I was grieving for Max Coyle, because I wasn't. What hit me was the fact of death itself: sudden, unexpected and final.

The scariest thing was that a member of this festive little house party had stabbed him and dumped his body, then carried on as if nothing had happened, looking the rest of us in the eye, making small talk, eating and drinking. That was what I couldn't take in.

'There's no chance it was someone from outside?' asked Holly, reading my thoughts. Then she answered her own question. 'No. That's clutching at straws.'

She was wrapped in a cream satin robe that matched her nightgown. Her feet were bare and her painted toenails the same pale pink as her manicure. She could have posed for

Vogue, right where she was. It was effortless with her. Even amid the shock, I registered my flannel pyjamas and sensible slippers and made a mental note to get something more presentable as soon as I got home.

'I was looking from face to face in the drawing room,' I said. 'It could be any of them. Max Coyle used information as a weapon. He hurt people. Who knows what secrets he was hoarding? We're aware of some, but I bet they're only the tip of the iceberg. Motives all over the shop.'

Everyone had gathered together after Donald and Andrew carried the body to the summer house. We couldn't call a doctor, or the police – they couldn't get here till the roads were cleared. We were marooned in a snow-bound house in the middle of nowhere with a dead body in the garden. Needless to say, the atmosphere in the drawing room was taut as a wire.

'Do your memory thing,' Holly urged. 'Tell me what you saw when we all came back in. Every detail.'

I closed my eyes for a minute and brought back the scene, like a snapshot in my head. The beautiful, bright room, the blazing fire, fairy lights reflected in the tall windows, red berries on the holly and white on the mistletoe, garlands of sweet pine and green ivy. The perfect Christmas setting. But there was no seasonal cheer in the faces around me, no laughter, no conversation. It was dinner time but no one had changed their clothes, no one was hungry. The MacRaes brought in a tray of steaming hot toddies and we sat like statues, drinking in heavy silence. Donald and Jean were calm and contained as they handed the drinks around, but something about their daughter caught my attention.

'Fiona seemed on edge.'

'What do you mean?'

'I can't say exactly. I mean, everybody was in shock, but she seemed wary. Jumpy. I caught Andrew watching her. He looked concerned.'

'She's like another daughter to him.'

'I think she's hiding something.'

'And Andrew knows?'

'Maybe.'

'What about his actual daughter? How did Ishbel look?'

'Subdued but calm. As you'd expect.'

'Well, I'm convinced she's another with a secret. What else do you remember? What about Esme?'

'White as a sheet. She found the body, of course.' Picturing her face, I sat forward in my chair. 'She looked scared to death.'

'She's been afraid all along. I wasn't wrong about that.'

'Could Max have been pursuing her?' I pondered. 'Like Dorothy? Threatening her career if she didn't comply?'

'I thought about that. But it seems unlikely. She is such an established star.'

'What could he know that would be damaging enough to force her to...'

I couldn't finish my sentence. The idea was so repulsive. I read the same disgust on Holly's face and then a sudden thought struck her.

'Perhaps he was threatening Andrew? What wouldn't Esme do to protect him?'

We lapsed into silence, considering the idea. After a while, I shook my head.

'I can't see Esme sticking a knife in anyone.'

'Can you see anyone here doing it?'

'Yes.' I surprised myself with how quickly my answer came. 'Elliot has it in him. And Sonya.'

'And Andrew, if it was to protect Esme.'

'Don't forget the men have been to war. They might all have killed already.'

'That's different.'

'Is it really, though?'

We've all seen too much death, more than other generations, more than those that come after us, I dearly hope. But I still felt shocked to the core by the sight of that silver blade thrust deep into a human neck. What would drive someone to do that? And how do you carry on living day to day with the knowledge of what you've done, the memory of the blood flowing and the light dying out of another person's eyes?

'Sonya seemed genuinely distraught.' Holly dragged me out of my dark thoughts. 'How did she look to you?'

I went back to the scene in my head.

'Shocked. Horrified.'

'What was Elliot doing? And why do you think he could kill Max?'

'I think he hated him with a passion. He masked it well but the look on his face sometimes...'

'You're right. I glimpsed it last night. He has a lot to hide, of course. As long as loving your own sex is illegal, men like Elliot are sitting targets for the unscrupulous.'

'He was paired with you on the search. How did he seem?'

'The same as always.'

'He seemed perfectly calm afterwards too, sitting with Dorothy on the sofa.'

'And Dorothy?'

I recalled Dorothy Drake, leaning back against the sofa cushions. What was that expression on her lovely face? I think I knew. It was relief. She was breathing easier now Max Coyle was dead.

'She volunteered to stay with Godfrey pretty sharpish,' said Holly. 'Maybe she knew what we'd find out there.'

'Maybe.'

Holly sat bolt upright, gripping the arms of her chair.

'What idiots we are!'

'What?'

'The murderer carried that dead weight through the snow. That eliminates most of the suspects! Dorothy couldn't do it. Esme or Ishbel couldn't. Or Sonya. Godfrey couldn't. Nor could Jean. I doubt that Elliot could. Or Fiona. Who does that leave?'

'Andrew, Donald,' I said. 'Ben.'

His name hung in the air between us.

'We have to consider him, darling.'

'Yes.'

'How did he look downstairs?'

I'd been trying not to think about him because, when I did, anxiety clutched at my heart like a vice. But I couldn't put it off any longer.

'He looked like a guilty man,' I said.

'What?'

'He couldn't meet my eyes.' I was clutching the cushion so

tightly my arms were aching. 'He's been quiet and a bit odd all day but after we found the body, he looked awful. Hunted.'

'Ivy?' There was a catch in Holly's voice. 'Seriously? You don't think your lovely Ben is a murderer?'

'He loathed Max Coyle.'

'So did most of the people here, darling.'

'You know he's a card-carrying communist? A real activist, not a wishy-washy socialist like me. He saw Max Coyle as a threat to everything he believes in. That's a motive, isn't it?'

He had fought hand to hand in Spain. How many fascists had he killed there? Would one more make a difference?

Holly looked unconvinced. 'I don't know, darling. This murder seems very personal.'

'He takes his politics very personally.' I made a Herculean effort to pull myself together, letting go of the cushion at last, replacing it in the corner of the chaise and smoothing out the creases. 'And he isn't *my* Ben.'

Holly just smiled.

'What?'

'I'll be here when you're ready,' she quoted.

'I wish I'd never told you.'

'He's yours if you want him.'

'Don't.'

'All right, darling. But don't let your emotions cloud your judgement. We're all behaving oddly at the moment. We're all in shock. I simply can't see Ben as a murderer.'

'He's one of three possible suspects if your theory is right.'

'But it isn't, now I think of it. It's full of holes. He could have been killed where he fell. Or perhaps the murderer had help.'

She threw up her hands. 'We don't know anything! We haven't the faintest clue who did it! Where do we start?'

My mind was spinning. Was it really only this morning that I walked to Bruce's Stone? Only 48 hours since we saw Black Gairy for the first time? It seemed like weeks. I took a deep breath.

'We're really doing this, then? Investigating a murder?'

'Well, I don't know about you, darling, but I can't just sit about waiting for the snow to stop and the phones to work. It could be days! We'll all be obsessing about it anyway. Might as well do it constructively.'

She was right. It was going to be a difficult few days, cooped up with a houseful of rattled people, imaginations working overtime and suspicions brewing like poison. Putting some method into the madness would help – having a purpose, even if it was self-imposed. Well, you wanted a different Christmas, Ivy, I told myself, and you got one. With knobs on.

'Fair enough,' I said. 'Let's have a go.'

She beamed at me. I wasn't sure if she was taking it seriously or casting herself as Miss Marple in a flight of fancy, but if we were going to do it, we'd do it properly. I demanded pen and paper and she supplied it.

'We need a plan of the house, whose room is where. Not that alibis will help, with most people sleeping alone.'

'We don't even know when he died.'

'No. But he never got to bed, as he was still in his evening clothes. So any time after three when he left Ben on the top landing. And before dawn as no one would carry a body about in daylight, would they? When does the sun rise?'

'About eight.'

'So a five-hour window. Where did he go? Who did he meet? We need a list of suspects and possible motives.'

'We need to talk to them all,' Holly enthused. 'One to one. Eye to eye. See if we sense anything or sniff anything out.'

'Your area of expertise.'

'It is, even if I say so myself. Then we can compare notes and select which leads to follow.'

She was definitely enjoying herself too much.

'We need a delicate approach,' I said firmly. 'No one must know what we're up to.'

'Of course, darling.'

I wasn't greatly reassured.

Together we roughed out a plan of Black Gairy and labelled the rooms and their occupants. There were nine bedrooms. Four singles on the top floor, occupied by Dorothy, Ben, Ishbel and Elliot. On the first floor, two doubles for Max and Sonya and Esme and Andrew, plus our suite. Then a single on the ground floor for Godfrey. All three MacRaes slept in the Lodge.

With that done, we made a list of names. Without Holly, me and the dead man, there were eleven. Next to each, we noted anything we knew or suspected so far.

> *Andrew Fergusson – ?*
> *Esme Arden – what is she afraid of?*
> *Ishbel Fergusson – secret?*
> *Donald MacRae – ?*
> *Jean MacRae – ?*
> *Fiona MacRae – worried about something*

Elliot Mayhew – hates Max. Why?
Dorothy Drake – harassed and threatened by Max
Godfrey Clifford – ?
Ben Newman – hates Max, behaving oddly
Sonya Stirling – betrayed wife

In black and white it looked like a load of nothing.

'Not much to go on.' I felt foolish, all of a sudden.

'We'll start fleshing it out tomorrow.'

'This is a mad idea.'

'Isn't it?' she laughed. 'All the best ones are.'

The general view of theatre people is that they're fluffy, silly creatures, too delicate for the real world, too soft for the hard knocks. In my experience, the opposite is true. Most of them are stout-hearted and adventurous. Uncrushable. Holly is all those things and I needed to be more like her.

I looked down at the eleven names, pictured their faces, and they looked back at me with all their secrets behind their eyes. One of them was hiding the biggest secret of all. Murder. And, with a bit of luck, me and Holly were going to uncover it.

18

Donald Macrae took a walk on the hills most days. To stretch his legs, he told Jean, but that wasn't the real reason. It was where he talked to his girls. He didn't believe in God or heaven, he knew he would never see them again, but under the wide sky, in the vastness of the landscape, he could feel them. It was strange that in a place they never visited, never even knew existed, he felt closer to them than anywhere else. He told them the everyday news, told them he loved them and missed them and, for a short time, the ache he carried constantly eased, the hole they had left in the world seemed smaller.

Standing in the snow in the thin morning light, he spoke out loud.

'You'll no guess what your wee sister has done the noo.'

Not that it mattered. Nothing she did could make a dent in his love for her and no threatened consequences would deter him from protecting her.

'There's no way we won't stand together. You canna break a bundle of sticks.'

A memory surfaced, a wave of joy and pain. Three small girls standing over a broken vase in the parlour, shamefaced but defiant, refusing to say which one of them was the culprit. They fought among themselves, silly squabbles and rivalries, but they always formed a united front against the world. He and Jean had taught them that. The power of numbers. Ten years on and he still caught himself looking either side of Fiona, expecting to see her sisters there, his three strong, bold girls, together again. But that would never be. All he had of them now were these moments, looking out at the water and the timeless hills and feeling them in his blood and bone.

He stayed longer than usual, reluctant to leave, but at last he headed down the hill to home. His heart was full and his face resolute. He had one daughter left and nothing would harm her whilst he had breath in his body.

19

HOLLY

I had vivid dreams. In one, Tom and I were standing on the shores of Loch Trool. The sun was bright on the water and the sky a sheet of vivid blue. I was my aging self and he was still twenty-four. It didn't matter at all.

'It's beautiful here,' he said to me. 'Don't let death cast a shadow.'

I woke up to see snow still falling outside the leaded windows. I had left the drapes pulled back when I went to bed so I could see the stars from my pillow and now the room was bright with morning light. For a few minutes, I felt Tom still with me, and it was lovely.

I stayed where I was, curled under the blankets, pondering his words. Did he mean his own death or Max Coyle's? I've tried hard not to let the loss of Tom overshadow me and mostly I've succeeded. Too many lives were thrown away as if they didn't matter. We owe it to them to acknowledge our good fortune and make the most of it. And what was poor Max Coyle owed? The guilty truth was I felt shock but no sorrow.

Precisely because I wasn't in mourning, I spent a long time, after my bath, selecting the most sombre clothes I'd brought with me, and at breakfast I could see that most of us had done the same. The atmosphere was subdued and awkward. Some looked more strained than others, but no one was really grieving, if you ask me, not even Sonya. She was drinking coffee and eating toast, looking lovely in a simple black dress, quieter than usual but otherwise calm.

I thought of the body lying cold and still in the locked summer house. How awful to be unloved and unmourned, to take all that life offered and use it to close hearts against you. How unutterably sad to be Max Coyle. In the absence of grief, perhaps we could give him the truth and find his killer? I could imagine the look Ivy would give me if I told her that. She'd say I was just finding a noble reason to enjoy myself and perhaps she'd be right.

I helped clear away after the meal and found myself alone in the kitchen with Esme. She was loading the dishwasher and humming softly to herself as she worked. 'Bewitched, Bothered and Bewildered' from *Pal Joey*. She had played Vera on Broadway just after the war and I'd managed to catch it between some filming days in New York. She was wonderful, as always.

'I loved you in that,' I said.

She looked up and smiled.

'Gene Kelly left the cast just as I joined. My biggest regret, missing him.'

'I'm sure he feels the same.' We laughed and, for a minute, life felt normal. But, of course, it wasn't. I watched Esme's face change as she remembered that too. 'I'm so sorry for what's happened in your beloved house.'

She shook her head, as if in disbelief. Keeping an eye on the door, she took my hand and leaned towards me.

'I was in such a state last night.'

'Hardly surprising.'

'No. It was foolish.'

I took the tea towel from her hands, clasped them both in mine and looked into her eyes.

'Are you going to tell me what's been troubling you? I know it has something to do with Max.'

'Was it so obvious?'

'I know you, darling. You were afraid of him.'

She sank into a chair at the table and I sat beside her, still holding her hands in mine. She was wearing a grey skirt and twinset with a single row of pearls and in the morning light from the kitchen window, she looked like a beautiful ghost, like she might fade and disappear before my eyes.

'He had a story. From my past. Before I knew you.'

So we were right. Max Coyle was like a spider at the centre of his web of information. How many lives had he menaced in his time? How many tortured souls were free now? No, I couldn't mourn him.

'You don't need to tell me, darling,' I said quietly.

'I don't mind you knowing. I made a fool of myself with a married man and his wife tried to kill herself. He was a public figure and there was quite a scandal, but I was lucky and my name was kept out of it. The mystery woman! Until Max found out.'

'And he was holding it over you?'

'I'm ashamed of it. That poor woman. I wasn't afraid for myself. I wouldn't have cared a fig if it wasn't for Andrew. But I couldn't bear for him to be dragged into the sordid mess.'

'And what did Max want for his silence?' I asked heavily. 'He was threatening to destroy Dorothy's career if she didn't sleep with him.'

111

'Oh, God.' She shook her head. 'No, nothing like that. He didn't demand anything. He just wanted me to know he knew. That he had proof. He enjoyed his power over me.'

'He was despicable.'

'In the end, I couldn't keep it from Andrew anyway. He knew there was something wrong and was imagining all sorts of horrors, so I told him everything. He was livid with Max. Wanted to throw him out of the house. I had to talk him out of it.' She gave me a wan smile. 'Of course, I wish I hadn't now. He'd still be alive.'

The image of Max's lifeless body lying in the snow flooded into my mind and I shuddered. Remembering Esme's terror at the discovery, I suddenly knew its cause.

'You thought Andrew had killed him,' I said.

Esme was always pale but now her lovely face was ashen.

'I saw the *sgian dubh* and thought of Andrew's fury at the man and, oh I don't know, once the idea was in my mind, it wouldn't go away.'

'But it wasn't Andrew's dagger?'

'I know. But all I could think was, "They'll hang him, they'll hang him."'

'Oh, darling.'

'Over and over in my head.'

'You don't still think—?' I began to ask.

'No. I came to my senses. It seems that Max was on the top landing harassing Dorothy at three in the morning, while Andrew was safely tucked up in bed with me. And I sleep lightly so I'm sure he didn't get up in the night.' She paused. 'Of course we don't know exactly when Max was killed.'

'Between three and eight in the morning seems most likely.'

'Well, Andrew has an alibi then. Me. What a hysterical idiot I was.'

'Ivy had a similar panic about Ben, if that makes you feel any better.'

'Why would Ben murder Max?'

'Politics.'

'What?'

'Ivy was no more rational than you, darling. We were all reeling last night.'

'But one of us did it, Holly. That's inescapable, isn't it?' She shivered. 'Someone I invited. That's what chills me to the bone.'

'No, no,' I said firmly. 'None of this is your fault, darling. Don't go down that road.'

'I can't help it.'

'Yes, you can. Don't punish yourself. And don't let it ruin Black Gairy for you. Choose not to do that. You must.'

She thought about what I said, looking around at the high walls and flagged floor and it seemed she was seeing through them to the rest of the house, to the wood and glass and stone that held us.

'Yes,' she said simply. 'You're right.'

'Of course I am.'

'Thank you.'

'My pleasure.'

She let go of my hand at last, gave me a hug and got to her feet.

'Better get on. The house party has been somewhat blighted but it still needs feeding.'

'We can fend for ourselves, darling.'

'No need. Jean is coming across soon to work her magic. I'll just finish loading the dishes. You go and put your feet up.' As I moved off, she turned from the sink. 'No one wanted him here but he just latched on. Poor Max. He should have stayed away.'

*

Andrew was standing by the hall table, phone in hand, frowning in irritation. He replaced the receiver as I passed.

'Lines still down. Bloody nuisance. We really need the police here as soon as possible.'

'Are the roads still blocked?'

'Worse than ever. Donald took a walk this morning and didn't get far. I'm considering a hike to Newton Stewart, where the nearest police are, but it's thirteen miles and no saying what the conditions are like.'

'It sounds risky.'

'Yes. But how long can we hang around doing nothing, with a body in the summer house?' His face was drawn. 'It's my home, Elspeth. My responsibility.'

'Do you know the weather forecast?'

'Yes, we still have the wireless, thank the Lord. It isn't encouraging. No sign of the snow stopping yet.'

'I assume they'll be working on the phone lines, even though it's Christmas?'

'I think that's likely.'

'Well, give them another day at least. Max isn't going anywhere, is he?'

He hesitated then nodded agreement.

'I'll re-assess tomorrow.'

'I think that's wise.'

'Thank you for the voice of reason.'

'Don't take all the weight of this on yourself.' I laid a hand on his arm. 'Yes. It's your house, but we're all in it together.'

He seemed to relax a little, even managed a slight smile.

'We're all going to lose our minds if we aren't careful. Esme found herself believing I'd killed him, for a while.'

'She told me.'

He looked at me closely.

'Did she tell you why?'

'Yes. Terrible man.'

'He traded in misery, it seems. And his poison still spreads after death. We're all looking at each other with suspicion.'

'I suppose it's inevitable.'

'I keep thinking what my grandfather would have made of all this. Black Gairy was a sanctuary for him, a symbol of all he'd achieved, somewhere almost sacred.' He looked at the door to the porch, as if seeing beyond it and outside the house. 'That range of hills around the loch is called the Awful Hand. I've always assumed it was awe as in wonderment.' His face clouded. 'It seems different now.'

*

In the dining room, Godfrey was sitting in his usual place by the French windows. He was holding an open book but not reading it, his head resting on the back of the chair, his eyes closed. I thought he was dozing and turned to leave but his voice stopped me.

'Coffee?'

He gestured to a steaming pot on the table by his side.

'Lovely.' I went to sit with him. Close up, he looked frail, overwhelmed by the large armchair. His hands were shaky as he poured me a cup and his face was drawn with exhaustion.

'You look worn out, Godfrey. Didn't you sleep?'

'Old age, my dear. I sleep very little these days. And today is a difficult day.'

'Yes. We're all feeling the strain.'

'Of course. Max.' He looked down at the pages of the book on his lap then up again. 'It's insensitive of me but I was thinking of something else. Forgive me.'

The sorrow in his eyes went straight to my heart. I sat forward and laid a hand on his arm.

'What is it, old friend? Can I help?'

'No, I'm afraid not. But thank you.' He gave me a sad little smile. 'It's Henrietta's birthday today.'

'Your daughter?'

'She would have been forty-five. I find it impossible to imagine that.'

'Oh, Godfrey.' I hesitated to go on but I felt he wanted to talk about her and, I confess, my curiosity got the better of me. 'You've never told me what happened to her.'

'A head injury. A riding accident. She was in a coma. I sat at her bedside for weeks. Waiting. Hoping.'

I felt my eyes fill with tears and swallowed them down as he tapped the book in his lap.

'*The Secret Garden.* It was her favourite when she was young. I was reading it to her when she slipped away.'

'I'm so sorry.'

'It was a long time ago.'

'That makes no difference.'

'You know that, of course.'

We sat together in silence for a while, drinking our coffee and looking out at the snow. Remembering.

Just out of sight, the summer house sheltered Max's body from the weather, not that it mattered to him anymore. I forced myself back to the present.

'How late did you sit up here the night Max died?'

Perhaps Godfrey had seen or heard something. Anything. A piece of the puzzle.

'Till about two, I think. When you all went up, Andrew, Max and I sat in here, having a nightcap. Max went out on the patio to smoke a cigar. Then Donald MacRae walked up from the lodge and Andrew went outside to have a word with him. After that, we all drifted off to bed.'

'Who first?'

'Andrew. Then I left Max finishing his drink. I assumed he went up soon after. I've learned since that he went to Dorothy's room, of course.' He gave a little frown of distaste. 'Luckily Ben was standing guard.'

'Ivy arranged it.'

'That doesn't surprise me at all.'

He offered me a refill of coffee and I accepted. I was glad to distract him if I could.

'Did you come back through to your chair during the night?'

It was a lame hope. As I expected, he shook his head.

'Not till dawn. Shortly after, Andrew came downstairs and out of the main door. Then Ivy, about half an hour later. And then Dorothy. Early morning walks, I presume.'

It all fitted with what we knew so far. Which was bugger all, as Ivy would say. Then a thought struck me.

'Why would Donald come to the house at that hour?'

'Yes. It seemed odd. But Max was still alive after that, so it can't be connected.' He looked hard into my face and seemed to read something there. 'You're on the case, I see.'

'What do you mean? I'm just curious. Who wouldn't be?'

'Who indeed?' He leaned forward. 'Well, here's a mystery for you. Before Donald appeared, the French windows were open slightly because Max was smoking and I heard a motorcar start up close by and drive away. What do you make of that?'

'A car?'

'There's no doubt.'

'At two in the morning? In this weather?'

'In the nick of time, I'd say. We were snowed in shortly afterwards.'

'Well, what on earth...?'

'Absolutely. See what Ivy makes of that when you compare notes.'

'We aren't—'

'And now, if you don't mind, my dear, I feel sleepy. I think I'll take a nap.'

'Godfrey!'

'Don't worry, Holly. My lips are sealed.'

I realised I was wasting my breath and let it go. He patted

my hand, leant back and closed his eyes. *The Secret Garden* was still open on his knees.

'Shall I take your book?'

'No.' He closed it and held it in both hands. 'I'll keep it with me.'

'Sweet dreams.'

I gave him a little kiss on his forehead and left him to his memories.

20

IVY

I was right about Dorothy. While everybody else was at least sobered by Max's death, she seemed lighter and more at peace than at any time since we arrived. She wasn't even trying to hide it.

'I'm glad he's dead and I don't care who knows it. No one here cared for him, not even his wife. Why pretend otherwise?'

We were in the library, toasting our toes by the fire. Dorothy had discovered an old gramophone and some records in the corner and put on an Al Bowlly song that took me right back to before the war, dancing with Sam on Saturday nights at the Floral Hall. As always now, thinking of Sam led me straight to Ben and I felt disloyal to Sam's memory. He deserved his own private place in my thoughts but, try as I might, Ben kept invading them.

He had eaten his breakfast and gone out for a walk before I was up and he wasn't back yet. After yesterday, I was fretting about how he would seem when I saw him again. The thought that he was avoiding me was nagging at the back of my mind but I kept pushing it away. Maybe Holly was right and I couldn't see straight where he was concerned, but I hadn't imagined his behaviour. Something was wrong. I had to have it out with him.

With an effort, I pulled my attention back to Dorothy.

'You didn't see the body,' I told her. 'You might feel differently if you had.'

'Maybe.'

'Aren't you wondering who did it?'

'Of course. But whoever it was, I don't blame them.'

Our conversation outside on Boxing Day came back to me then. There was something she wasn't telling me. What had she meant, playing Max at his own game?

'If you don't mind me saying, you'd be a prime suspect in any investigation. Strong motive and all that.'

I don't know what I expected but it wasn't that she would burst out laughing.

'Stab him with a fancy dagger and drag him through the grounds in the pitch dark and snow? Not likely. I'd have put something in his drink and let him die in his bed. So much easier.'

It was the first time I'd seen her laugh out loud and I got a glimpse of the real person under the charm school veneer: less polished, less cautious, altogether livelier. They had removed some personality along with her rough edges and, by the looks of it, that was a shame. At any rate, whatever she was hiding, I was pretty sure I wasn't looking at a guilty conscience.

'Who do you think did it then?'

'If you ask me, it was Sonya. She believed he was having an affair with me and that was the last straw. Ironic that he was killed for the one thing he didn't do.'

'Not for want of trying.'

'That's true.' She shuddered. 'He was a horrible man. I think I might have killed him if I was married to him. I hope she gets away with it.'

*

Sonya didn't look guilty. I know I told Holly that she was capable of murder – there is something a bit Medea about her – but seeing her sitting on the window seat in the drawing room, looking out at the falling snow, it seemed beyond belief that she would plunge a knife into Max's neck, however much she hated him. I realised that I was still a bit star-struck, that she was still larger than life in my eyes, in spite of everything that had happened. When she caught me staring, I felt myself blush.

'Sorry to disturb you.'

'Not at all. I'm glad of the company. Come join me.'

I sat beside her in the wide window bay and searched for something to say.

'Will it ever stop snowing?' It was the best I could come up with. Pathetic.

'I made a movie once about a family trapped by the weather in a haunted house.'

'*Terror in the Snow*.'

'You saw it?' She gave me a wry smile. 'Not one of my best. But I can't stop thinking about it. Life imitating art, as they say.'

'There are no ghosts here.'

'Aren't there?' She glanced around the room and then back at me. 'I keep seeing him. Sitting in a chair. Crossing the hall. Climbing the stairs. And always in that ridiculous outfit he was so proud of. The Coyle tartan. What vanity!'

'How long were you married?'

She looked me straight in the eyes. Hers were green and long lashed and sharp with intelligence.

'That isn't what you want to know. You want to ask why I married him in the first place. Why, in the name of all that's holy, did I marry a man like him? Am I right?'

'It is a bit of a puzzle.'

She laughed.

'Holly says you're a straight talker. I like it.' She nodded towards the decanters on the drinks table. 'Shall we have a wee dram, as they say in these parts?'

It was eleven o'clock in the morning but I didn't want to put a damper on things so I nodded and she poured us both generous doubles. Twelve-year-old single malt, amber and peaty, like the warm remnants of a wood fire in a glass. I swirled and sipped whilst Sonya knocked hers back like a pro and helped herself to a refill.

'Money. That's why. Obscene amounts of money.'

'Didn't you have enough of your own?'

'There you go again. Good for you, Ivy. But no, I didn't.' She sat, cradling her glass, long, slim fingers and an elegant French polish. 'I was in a legal battle with the studio, to get out of my contract.'

'I remember that.'

She was the first female star to take on the might of Hollywood. The men in suits. Very expensive suits. Most people thought she was mad to try. Whatever she was, Sonya Stirling wasn't short of guts.

'It had drained me dry and the bastards were relying on their deeper pockets to force me out of court. I wasn't going to let that happen, oh no, not when a multi-millionaire was in the market for a trophy wife and happy to pay for one. I won my case and I figured if I was prepared to marry a bastard to do it then we probably deserved each other.'

'So you never loved him?'

'Ivy, my girl, I never even liked him.'

It was a sad story. Sonya Stirling, adored by millions, who must have had her pick of countless lovesick suitors, ending up with a husband she despised and thinking so little of herself that she accepted it as her just desserts. All those years I stared up at her on the screen. Admired her. Envied her. What do they say about never getting to know your idols?

'I'm sorry.'

'No need. How shall I put it? We both found solace elsewhere.'

'But you were angry about Dorothy.'

'I was livid. But that was because he was doing it in plain sight. Our arrangement strictly outlawed that and he was tearing it up in public.' She read my thoughts which were probably clear as day. 'Some motive, eh? But here's the thing. It wasn't me.'

'Well, you would say that, wouldn't you?'

She laughed again.

'I suppose I would. But believe me or not, Ivy, I didn't kill him. I'd had enough, for sure, but I was planning divorce, not murder. Before someone else in this lovely house saved me the trouble.'

She was convincing. But she was Sonya Stirling. Trust me to try and solve a mystery in a house full of actors.

*

I left Sonya to her whisky and went in search of a cup of tea. The kitchen smelt gorgeous. Baking bread. There was a large teapot on the table and all three MacRaes were sitting round it, heads together, deep in talk which stopped as I walked in. A brief moment of awkwardness was broken by Donald, who smiled and indicated the pot.

'Just brewed. Would you like a cup?'

'Please.'

I hesitated. Jean looked welcoming enough but Fiona could barely meet my eyes. What the hell was going on there?

She stood up abruptly. 'Take my chair. I better get on.'

With a nod to her parents, she was gone. Jean and Donald must have noticed her odd behaviour, but they carried on as if nothing had happened, pouring my tea and fetching milk.

'Will you have a piece of cake?'

Jean brought me a generous chunk of Christmas cake and I tucked in. It still felt such a treat to have the things that we took for granted before the war and though rationing was easing, it was far from over, so I was making the most of all this plenty whilst I could, like a kid in a sweet shop. Like everyone else, I'd been in no mood for dinner after we found the body but the lack of appetite hadn't lasted long. The shock was dissipating and there was no grief to take its place. Poor Max.

'How are you feeling today?' Donald picked up on my thoughts.

'Better than last night.'

'Aye. It's an awful business.'

'To think of him lying there in the snow all day.' Jean shook her head. 'I'll not pretend I liked him, Miss Earnshaw. He was everything I despise—'

'Now then, Jean.'

'Och, you know it's true. But I wouldna wish that on anybody.'

Donald threw me an apologetic look.

'Jean speaks her mind.'

'Don't worry,' I smiled. 'I've been accused of that more than once myself.'

'Why leave him there, though? Where a search would find him? It makes no sense.'

Remembering my walk to the loch, I turned to Donald.

'Do you lock the gates at night?'

'Aye. Last thing.'

'What time was that on Christmas night?'

'Just after midnight.'

'But Max was still alive and well at three o clock.'

Jean sat forward, understanding dawning in her face. 'The killer tried to take the body away but couldna get out.'

'So it was dumped close till there was a chance to move it, but the opportunity didn't arise in time.'

'That makes sense.'

'Imagine joining the search, knowing what was there and waiting for it to be found.' Jean shook her head. 'Doesna bear thinking about.'

'It's a shocking thing to happen at the auld house. Not the Christmas you signed up for, Miss Earnshaw.'

'You can say that again. And please, it's Ivy. You're right, though. Something so ugly seems doubly wrong in this setting.'

'It's a special place, right enough.'

'It is. How long have you lived here?

I saw a change in their faces as I spoke, a shared sadness. I remembered what Holly had told me about their daughters and I could have kicked myself. Jean reached for Donald's hand before she answered.

'We've been here nearly ten years. We stayed in Clydebank all our lives till we were bombed out and Andrew offered us the lodge.'

'We needed a fresh start, a new life.' Donald was cradling Jean's hand in both of his. 'We lost two of our girls that day. Fiona is all we have now.'

There was an ocean of sorrow in their eyes and I could have bitten my tongue off for raising the subject, waking such pain.

'I'm so sorry.'

'You lost your husband in the war, didn't you?' Jean asked and I nodded. 'Then you know.'

'Nothing is quite the same afterwards, is it?' Donald looked at me with a new intimacy now, a shared experience of loss. 'My life had been the shipyard, the union and politics for thirty years and overnight, it all meant nothing. I left it without a backward glance.'

'I'd be a librarian in Morecambe if Sam was still alive.'

'You walked away too. Do you miss any of it?'

'My family. The sea. What about you?'

'The camaraderie. There was a great spirit in the yards. And in the party.'

'The SNP?'

'No, lassie. The Communist Party.' He indicated Jean. 'We were both members.'

Like Ben. This Christmas party had more than its fair share of revolutionaries. What were the odds on that?

'But not anymore?' I asked.

'The party is torn,' Jean said. 'Some want a British Communism but some are still loyal to Russia, whatever Stalin does. We couldna go along with that.'

'We supported Willie Gallacher. Helped get him into parliament. But he lost his seat this year.' Donald topped up my tea and offered more cake but I exerted some willpower and shook my head. 'There are no Communist MPs now. Some comrades have joined Labour or the SNP but I don't think we'll get so involved again. What about you, Ivy?'

'Labour family,' I told them. 'Born and bred. I'm not a member though. I'm all for politics but, with a few honourable exceptions, I'm not so fond of politicians.'

'Credit where it's due, mind,' said Donald. 'Labour have done great things since the end of the war. There's been real change for working people.'

'And what's their reward?' I asked. 'They scraped a majority in the election this year. The Tories will be back in no time and they'll wipe it all away.'

'Aye,' Jean nodded. 'The system is set up to preserve the status quo.'

'But we're a' Jock Tamson's bairns.'

Jean read my face and smiled. She leaned across the table to pat my hand.

'He means we're all equal.'

'"A man's a man for a' that,"' I said, quoting from Holly's Christmas present. They both beamed at me.

'I'll be honest,' Donald chuckled. 'I didnae expect to find comrades at a house party like this one.'

'Oh but we're show business, not gentry. We're from all walks of life. And, I have to say, from my experience, Max Coyle was the exception not the rule.'

Max's name was like a wet blanket on our cosy chat as we were all reminded of our reality. I'm sure we were all seeing the same awful image in our minds.

'It's a terrible thing to happen to anybody,' said Donald at last.

Jean got to her feet and started clearing the table. It was the longest I'd ever seen her sit still. Busying herself again, she spoke over her shoulder, her voice solemn.

'The man had a lot to answer for. His sins came home to roost.'

It was harsh but true. Max Coyle had come to Black Gairy for Christmas with no idea, until it was too late, that one sin in a lifetime of sins was about to catch up with him there and put an end to his sinning forever.

*

Elliot was leaning on the gallery rail above the hall, exactly where we had first seen him when we arrived on Christmas Eve. He summoned me with a lazy finger and I went up to join him where the light from the vast stained-glass window behind us dappled him with green and yellow. A Saville Row suit, handmade shirt, silk tie, Italian shoes and every hair in place, he looked elegant, affluent and conspicuously unruffled by events.

'Everyone else has the grace to look pensive, at least,' I said to him as I approached. 'Are you really so unaffected by it all?'

'On the contrary, dear girl. I'm cock a hoop. The world is a better place this morning.'

'Harsh.'

'But true.'

'Why did you hate him so much?'

He raised an eyebrow.

'You met him, didn't you?'

'I know. He was a nasty piece of work. But it was more than that for you.'

'Yes, it was.'

'So?'

'Ivy, darling. There are things I'm not prepared to share, even with you.'

'But...'

'Change the subject, poppet. You won't move me on this.'

'All right.' I looked over the balustrade into the panelled hall, decked with lights and greenery, the star on the top of the tall Christmas tree so high I could almost touch it from the first floor. The scent of pine was familiar and comforting. I thought of Mum and Dad's little house and the home-made wreath on the front door that greeted me every year when I walked up the path, weighed down with presents and warm with expectation. I should have stuck with tradition, spent Christmas there and stayed well away from this beautiful house full of ugly secrets.

'Penny for them,' drawled Elliot.

I was tired of him suddenly, tired of the game.

'There's a murderer here. You might be able to rise above it but I can't. It bothers me.'

He registered the mood change and was silent for a minute. When he spoke, his flippancy was gone, his tone serious.

'And what if the killer wasn't one of the party? What if someone else was here on Christmas Day?'

'It's a comforting theory but—'

'No buts. I saw someone.'

'What?'

'A young woman. She was in the trees, near the little shed behind the lodge.'

'When?'

'About four o'clock in the afternoon. At the time I assumed it was the girl from the village who was supposed to come and help with the dinner.'

'Morag Murray.'

'Yes, but she cancelled because of the snow, so it wasn't her.'

'Then who was it?'

'Who knows? And was she alone? There might have been an entire coach party sneaking about the place.' He gave me a sardonic smile. 'At any rate, it blows apart your morbid theory that the murderer was definitely at our table.'

He was right. There was a real possibility that Max's killer had come and gone before we found his body. In one way, it was a relief but for our investigation, it was an added complication. One step forward, two steps back. This detective business was harder than it looked.

21

Sonya Stirling trudged up the snow-covered slope to the summer house and walked around the back where she couldn't be seen from Black Gairy. She had more right than anyone to look through the window at her husband's dead body, but still she felt self-conscious and didn't want to be observed.

The still, white mound laid out on one of the benches inside seemed small for a man who had cast such a large shadow while he lived. That's a lesson, Sonya told herself. Death is the great leveller. Dispassionately, she examined her heart for any sign of grief but found none. She wasn't sorry he was dead and had no regret for what she had done. She had always taken responsibility for her actions and this time was no different. It was a shame to drag good people into her mess, but they'd get over it.

Turning away, she looked out over the gardens to the loch and mountains beyond. The winter sun reflected on the icy water, dappling the snow through the bare branches. It was picture postcard perfect, she thought. Except for the corpse in the cute wooden building behind her.

Smiling at her own cynicism, she headed back to the house. Time for a long soak before dinner. She had needed to see Max's body as a kind of test, and she had passed. She was at peace with herself. She wasn't scared. Even though her fate was yet to be decided, she still had options. It wasn't over till it was over.

22

HOLLY

'Right,' I said. 'Where's the list we made last night? I have updates.'

'Me too.' Ivy produced the paper from her handbag and I grabbed a pen.

I had found her talking to Elliot on the galleried landing and whisked her away with some excuse about fixing a zip before we went down for lunch. We were sitting in our usual places by the window in my room and I was dying to tell her what I'd discovered and hear all the news from her.

'I'll start. I spoke to Esme first. You were right about her being terrified. She thought Andrew had done it.'

'Why?'

'Max was tormenting her with a news story from her past. Holding it over her for kicks.'

'Nice man.'

'She thought Andrew had snapped and stabbed him.'

'Well, someone did.'

'Yes. But it wasn't Andrew. Esme gave him an alibi for three o'clock onwards. In bed with her. Make a note of that.'

Ivy dutifully recorded it and everything else I told her, then she reported her morning's work. When we'd finished, we looked back over the list of names and the new information:

Andrew Fergusson – *nightcap with Max and Godfrey. Spoke to Donald on patio around 2am. Esme believed he'd done it but has changed her mind. She says they were in bed together by 3am. He seems determined to contact police. Would a guilty man be so keen? Or is it a bluff?*

Esme Arden – *If she did it, she would know Andrew was innocent but her fear for him seemed genuine. Double bluff? They alibi each other for 3am onwards.*

Donald MacRae – *Says he locked gates just after midnight. Is that why the body wasn't taken out of the grounds? Came up to patio and spoke to Andrew soon after Godfrey heard car. Why would he do that so late at night? If there was a car, who let it out and locked up after it?*

Jean MacRae – *Disliked Max but seemed shocked by murder.*

Fiona MacRae – *Avoiding Ivy. Why?*

Elliot Mayhew – *Happy Max is dead. Admits he loathed him. Won't say why. Says he saw a stranger in the grounds on Christmas Day afternoon. A young woman.*

Dorothy Drake – *Glad Max is dead. Thinks Sonya did it.*

Godfrey Clifford – *Had nightcap with Max and Andrew. Saw Donald chat with Andrew on terrace. Heard a car start up and drive away around 2am. Says Andrew went up shortly afterwards. Left Max downstairs when he went to bed.*

Sonya Stirling – *Admits she was furious at Max's behaviour. Married for money and never loved him. Says he never came to their room on Christmas night.*

'More than we had,' I said, 'but it's all still a muddle, isn't it?'

'We still need to talk to Ishbel and Fiona.'

'What about Ben?'

'Still avoiding me.'

I hesitated, choosing my words very carefully. 'Ivy, my darling. Is it possible his behaviour might have nothing to do with the murder? That there's another reason why he might be feeling uncomfortable around you?'

I watched her face change. It broke my heart to see it.

'Oh. You think he's having second thoughts?'

'I don't know.'

'But you said—'

'I know. He seemed so smitten. But stranger things have happened. I'm just looking at all possibilities.'

She looked at me bleakly. 'I don't know which suspicion is worse.'

I went over to the chaise and gave her a hug.

'I'm sorry, my darling. I expect you'd forgotten what a minefield love affairs can be.'

I was taken back to the first time I saw her, in the quick change booth behind the set of *Lady Windermere's Fan*, at the Morecambe Alhambra. The rain was thundering on the roof and her hair was wet from her walk to the theatre. She was so young. So broken. I looked in her eyes and saw myself.

Two wars. Two widows. Well, I never actually got down the aisle but that makes no difference. Tom in the Flanders mud, Sam under the waters of the Norwegian Sea. I saw my pain fresh minted in Ivy and it showed me how far I'd come since my loss. I was determined to convince her that the darkness wasn't forever and that she had a future. 'What wound did ever heal but by degrees?' All our years since sprang from that common ground. Whether or not our meeting that night was destiny or happenstance, I'm so grateful for it. I know it's a tired old cliché but she's like the daughter I never had. I want so much for her.

'We don't know anything for certain,' I said. 'We're just guessing, aren't we? Let's keep an open mind till we know more.'

'Easier said than done.'

'Do you want to take a break? We can do this later.'

'No.' She gave herself a shake. 'Not a bit. Let's carry on.'

I stood up and walked to the window, looking out at the white world outside. The snow was still swirling, but I focused on the trees beyond the lawns, the dark mass that had hidden Max's body from sight while we carried on oblivious in the warmth and light of the house.

'Two things stand out for me,' I said. 'The young woman Elliot saw and the car Godfrey heard.'

'Yes. I agree.'

'Could Elliot have been mistaken about the stranger in the grounds?' I asked. 'No one else mentioned seeing her.'

'Or did he invent her to avert suspicion?'

'He did look genuinely puzzled when Esme said the Morag girl had cancelled. I didn't understand why at the time, but it makes sense now.'

'Well, if she was real, who was she?'

I threw myself back into my chair. There were too many questions and not enough answers.

'And was that her car leaving at two in the morning? Godfrey was sure he heard it and I've no reason to doubt him.'

It was Ivy's turn to get up. She paced the room for a while, saying nothing. I could almost hear her mind working.

'It does widen the suspect pool, like Elliot said. If she was here, could there be others?' She shook her head, answering her own question. 'No. I don't buy it. Do you?'

'Perhaps that one young lady. But more than that is hard to imagine.'

'Aye. Let's stick with what we know, not invent more problems.'

I watched her cross in front of me and back again. At last I had a new thought.

'Somebody had to open the gates to let that car out.'

She stopped in her tracks. 'That's right. Who would have access to keys? The MacRaes. Andrew and Esme. Anyone else?'

'I doubt it.'

'Andrew was with Godfrey at the time,' she said. 'Esme had gone to bed, she says, but we only have her word for it. Donald only came up to the patio afterwards, so he was free to do it. So was Jean. But they didn't mention it when we talked about locking up. Why not, if there was an innocent explanation?'

'Unless it was Fiona?'

'Has she been acting strangely around you too?'

'I don't know. I haven't seen her.'

'You need to talk to her. Find out what she's hiding.'

'That's my next job then. What about Ishbel? There's a mystery there and I would put money on it featuring boyfriend Jack.'

'Absolutely. But what though?' Returning to the chaise, Ivy stretched out in her usual pose, running a hand through her dark curls without a thought to her coiffure. 'Maybe he's a married man?'

'I don't think so. He's a student with her at Glasgow. But there's something amiss there, I'm sure of it.'

'A student at Glasgow...' she repeated.

'Yes. What?'

I could see her mind making connections. 'Politics students. What did Max call them when he was talking about the Stone being stolen? A hotbed of nationalism.'

'Something unpleasant. Naturally.'

Ivy sat up. Her curls were standing on end rather comically and she was smiling from ear to ear.

'I've had a mad thought.'

'Share it, my darling.'

'Brace yourself. What if, instead of enjoying the hospitality at Black Gairy, Ishbel's Jack was driving a Ford Anglia from London to Scotland with the Stone of Destiny in the boot?'

I stared at her in shock and delight. It was a glorious idea.

'This house is very handy for the border,' I said.

'What if the car Godfrey heard was carrying two students with a very special cargo?'

'And Elliot saw one of them in the grounds.'

'It's a stretch,' she laughed. 'But wouldn't it be brilliant if it's right?'

'It would be thrilling. How do we find out?'

She was on her feet again. We were both buzzing with excitement.

'You need to grill Ishbel. Do your actressy thing and she might let her guard down.'

'Actressy thing?'

'All frothy and chatty and charming. You know what I mean.'

'I suppose I do.'

'No offence meant.'

'None taken.'

'And ask Fiona what she knows about Jack. They're in different departments but she might have met him, through Ishbel.'

'Roger. Over and out. What will you do?'

Ivy came to a standstill and I watched the joy die out of her face. I knew what she was going to say.

'I need to have a conversation with Ben.'

'I'm sorry, darling, but you do.'

She nodded. 'I'll find him now.'

'Screw your courage to the sticking place,' I said.

I was silently cursing Ben Newman. If he was toying with my girl, if he had given her false hope and hurt her, he would have me to deal with and in that case, he might be better off confessing to murder!

23

Elliot Mayhew was standing outside the door to Sonya and Max's room, staring at the handle and willing himself to turn it. Again and again he looked along the landing to the stairs, checking that no one was coming. He had seen Sonya leave the house and shortly afterwards, Holly had gone downstairs where, by his calculations, all the others were in one room or another. He was as safe as he could be.

'Get on with it,' he chided himself.

He reached out a hand, holding his breath. If the room was locked, this was all for nothing. But the knob turned and the door opened. Dizzy with nerves, he slipped inside and closed it behind him, leaning against the wood, trying to steady his breathing. His eyes swept the room and he saw what he was looking for almost immediately. Max's leather briefcase was propped against the bedside table. Grasping it in a shaking hand, he opened the door a crack and peeped out into the corridor. The coast was clear. He was up the stairs to the second floor and in his room in seconds.

He turned the key in the door, dropped the case onto his bed and sank into the armchair, weak with relief. He was safe now to search for what he hoped to find. It was a long shot but there was a chance Max carried it around with him. Worth a try, anyway. Worth the risk.

Leaning forward, he pressed the two catches with trembling hands and then his heart sank. The lid stayed fast shut. The case was locked. Of course a man like Coyle would take no chances with his private property.

No doubt the key was somewhere in the bedroom, in a drawer or a pocket, but he couldn't go back there. He didn't have the courage. Or perhaps it was still on Max's body? Elliot shuddered. No. The key was out of reach. If he wanted to see inside, he would have to break it open.

It was an expensive briefcase with a sturdy lock. He tried a nail file, a letter opener and a large pair of scissors he found in the dressing table drawer. None of them worked. He hit it with a stone paperweight, with the heel of his shoe and then with the poker, which finally did the trick. With a quickening heart, he raised the lid and rifled through the papers inside. His heart sank. He searched twice but what he wanted wasn't there. Dropping the lid shut, he threw himself back in the armchair and closed his eyes.

He wouldn't feel free until it was back in his hands. With Max Coyle dead, the immediate threat was lifted but the anxiety lingered, eating at him, destroying his peace. Coyle couldn't hurt him anymore, but others could, if they wanted to. And there would always be others. Life had taught him that much.

24

HOLLY

Ishbel was in the drawing room and there was no one with her. I descended on her like a ship in full sail and she politely closed the magazine she was leafing through and gave me her attention. The wireless was on in the background and the velvet voice of Nat King Cole serenaded us softly with 'Mona Lisa' as we talked. She looked very young, simply dressed in black slacks and a mauve sweater with her hair tied back and no make-up.

'How are you bearing up?' I asked as I sat down.

'I'm fine. Better than I should be, I suppose. It's heartless, I know, but I can't bring myself to care about Max Coyle. He was a monster.' She gave me a wry smile. 'Shocking, isn't it? The youth of today. I mean, I'm sorry for his family and for the shock everyone is feeling, but that's all.'

'I can't bring myself to disagree with you there.' I leaned forward and lowered my voice. 'But doesn't it worry you that you're trapped in a snowbound house with a murderer?'

'Are we? He could have gone out to meet someone we don't know about. Or one of the hundreds of people he's hurt over the years could have tracked him down and killed him.'

Ivy and I had already dismissed that theory and, I think, wisely. I gave Ishbel a wry smile.

'In a snowstorm in the middle of nowhere?'

'But nothing is certain, is it?'

I decided to take a risk and drop a little bombshell. 'Godfrey heard a car leaving the grounds in the early hours.'

I was disappointed. She looked interested but there was no sign of guilt or panic in her face.

'I wonder who it was?'

'I thought maybe your Jack had paid a sneaky visit,' I said, with a big, jokey smile, watching her closely. And there it was. Talking about Jack made her uncomfortable. That much was certain. 'But why would that have to be a secret? Silly me.'

'I wish you were right.' There was an edge to her voice. She knew I was prying and resented it. 'But Jack is having a family Christmas, hundreds of miles away, in Devon.'

'His family aren't in Scotland?'

'No. Why would they be? They're English.'

'My mistake. I had assumed he was a Scot. Because he's at Glasgow. There I go, leaping to conclusions again.'

'There are lots of non-Scots there.'

'Of course. I suppose it was Max saying how the place was full of nationalists...'

It was clumsy, but I couldn't help myself. I held my breath, waiting for her reaction.

'Ah yes, the hotbed of independence.'

It was a complete anticlimax. She was faintly amused, but nothing more.

'Don't you agree with them? You gave Max a run for his money on the subject.'

'I just wanted to puncture his pomposity. I don't have strong feelings about it. I leave that to Fiona.'

'Fiona MacRae?'

'She's a real believer. Don't get her started on it if you haven't got time to listen.' She paused, looking thoughtful. 'I'm not even sure that I feel Scottish. I grew up in England and went to school there. My mother was English. And Jack and I will probably live there after graduation. I think, if Scotland wants independence, it should have it, but I hardly feel qualified to have an opinion.'

So much for our wild suspicions! It seemed Jack was out of the picture. But I was reluctant to abandon the marvellous Stone theory and perhaps it wasn't quite dead and buried yet. We had Fiona to consider now.

Gordon Jenkins had succeeded Nat King Cole on the wireless, wishing Irene goodnight too many times for my liking. He was followed by the 'Third Man Theme', which made me smile to myself. Much more in keeping with the job at hand. Which, if I say so myself, I am rather good at. People talk to me. They always have.

Having asked what I'd wanted to, I allowed myself to go off at a tangent.

'I know your mother died when you were very young. I'm sorry.'

'I was only four. I barely remember her. Which saddens me. There are photographs, of course, and Dad always talked about her to me, kept her memory alive, but that's not the same, is it?'

'No, it isn't. What was her name?'

'Madeleine.'

'I'm so sorry for what you missed. And that Madeleine missed seeing what a lovely young woman you've become.'

'Thank you.' She smiled. 'Dad says I look a lot like her. That pleases me.'

'You're very close to your father, aren't you?'

'For a while all we had was each other.'

'Of course.'

'I'm glad he found Esme though. I can spread my wings without worrying about him.'

'Even when tycoons end up dead in his garden?' I laughed.

'Even then. They'll weather the storm. They'll be fine.'

I didn't know if she was trying to convince me or herself but I nodded along anyway and hoped she was right. Ivy and I were indulging ourselves, but the snow had to stop eventually and then the police would come, an arrest would be made and someone would hang for the murder of Max Coyle. After that, could Black Gairy ever feel the same again?

25

IVY

I found him in the library. There was a book in his hand but he wasn't reading it. He was standing by the window and turned with a start when I walked in. The blood rushed into his face then drained out again. He couldn't even manage a smile. I checked there was no one else in the room, then closed the door and leant against it.

'Are you going to tell me what's wrong?'

He looked at the book as if he hadn't realised it was there then dropped it on a table. I waited, my heart beating a tattoo in my chest. The silence was unbearable.

'Ben?'

He let out a breath slowly. He still couldn't bring himself to look at me.

'I don't want to lie to you.'

'Don't, then.'

'Yesterday was hell. I thought I could do it, just carry on. But I can't.'

Cold dread washed over me. Was he talking about murder or love? Either way, my fledgling romance was over before it really began.

'What are you talking about?'

'I'm trying to protect you.'

'What? I don't need protecting.'

'You don't know.'

'Tell me, then. Explain.'

'I can't.'

I was upset but I was also fast losing patience. Where did he get off, coming into my life, turning it upside down, then pulling away like this? I pushed off from the door and stood upright, on my own two feet, like I always have, like I always will.

'Did you murder Max Coyle?' I asked him flatly.

I couldn't read his face at all. I wished Holly was there to help.

'No,' he said quietly. 'I didn't.'

'Do you think I murdered him?'

'What? No. Of course not.'

'So why can't you talk to me?'

He turned away and dropped into a chair, as if he didn't have the wherewithal to stay upright any longer.

'I made a mistake.'

Was he confessing indifference to me or to murder? I wanted to shake him. I wanted to cry.

'I thought we were starting something,' I said. 'If you don't want that now, at least have the guts to say so.'

He winced like I'd hit him and I felt a rush of guilt but I didn't give in to it. He owed me an explanation. I forced myself to wait through the silence, with my heart thumping and the blood rushing in my ears. Finally he spoke, his voice so low I could barely hear it.

147

'You know how I feel about you.'

'I don't. I don't know anything. You're lying to me.'

'I haven't lied.'

'I don't trust you.'

He raised his eyes to mine at last. They were wide with pain. It broke my heart.

'I deserve that,' he said simply. 'And I don't know how to change it.'

There was nothing more to say. I shook my head, turned my back and walked out.

26

HOLLY

We met on the landing. I was going down as Ivy was coming up. She looked ghastly. Clearly her talk with Ben hadn't gone well. When she told me, I wanted to march up to him and give him a piece of my mind, but she made me swear not to.

'Not till I'm clearer in my head. Promise?'

'I promise. Reluctantly.'

She was pale and on the verge of tears. I wrapped my arms around her.

'What shall we do? Go for a walk? Get drunk?'

She gave me a watery smile.

'If you don't mind, I'd like a bit of time on my own.'

'Of course, darling. Off you go and have a big cry. It always helps. There are some chocolate limes left in my bedside drawer. I'll come up and see you soon.'

It was hard to keep my word, watching her climb the stairs as if she had the weight of the world on her shoulders. How full of briars is this working-day world!

What was Ben playing at? I couldn't bring myself to believe he had killed Max and I'd been so sure that he was smitten with Ivy, so what was making him drive a wedge between them? What secret was he carrying? I took a few steps towards the library door, then forced myself to turn back. It had been a solemn promise. For now I'd have to look elsewhere for answers.

I'd given myself the job of interviewing Fiona but a quick search confirmed that she wasn't in the house, so that had to wait. I wandered into the drawing room where Dorothy and Elliot were playing cards. The wireless was on and I sank into a chair by the fire, giving half an ear to the news, watching the flames curl around the logs piled high in the hearth.

'Do you want to join us?' Elliot called over.

'No, thank you, darling. Feeling too lazy.'

It wasn't true but I couldn't tell them I was too busy playing detective, that my head was too full of questions and theories to play Gin Rummy.

When the news came on, I listened for anything more on the Stone of Destiny. At first the report was more of the same – the Dean of Westminster had called the theft an act of sacrilege; the theory that nationalists had taken it seemed to be generally accepted now and a nationwide search was underway, concentrating on routes to the north. Then there was something new. It was suspected that the young couple seen by the policeman had split up to avoid suspicion and they were now looking for information on any young women driving alone to Scotland on Christmas Day and Boxing Day.

My mind whirled. What time did Elliot see the mysterious young woman in the grounds? How long does it take to drive from Westminster Abbey to Loch Trool? Was it all about the Stone after all? I really needed to talk to Fiona.

Another foray into the kitchen revealed Jean and Donald busy with dinner preparations, but no sign of their daughter. If she was down at the lodge, that could be the perfect opportunity to get her on her own. A bit cheeky to roll up and knock on the door but hey ho, in for a penny. I donned coat, boots and hat and sallied forth on my mission.

For once it wasn't actually snowing and it might have been my imagination but the air felt different. Was the weather finally changing? About time. Though the drive was clear, the snow was several feet deep in places off the path, with great drifts of white piled up against the trees and weighing down the branches till they almost touched the ground. It was thick on the sloping roof of the lodge too and on the deep sills below the leaded lights of the windows. A row of delicate icicles hung from the eaves like Christmas decorations, and a curl of smoke rose from the stone chimney. It was like a scene from a fairy tale.

Then I remembered the darkness at the heart of those old stories. I shivered and it wasn't from the cold. The reality of the murder, of what I was doing, hit me suddenly, standing there at the lodge door, and I lowered my raised hand and took a step back. This isn't a play, I told myself. This is real life. What are you doing?

'Hello.'

I nearly jumped out of my skin! Fiona was coming through the open gates, looking at me with curiosity and some suspicion. I gathered myself and flashed my most dazzling smile.

'Hello. I was looking for you. Have you got a few minutes to talk?'

At first, I thought she was going to refuse but then she

nodded and led the way indoors, into a cosy little sitting room with crowded bookshelves, a gramophone next to a stack of records and a Bakelite wireless set in the corner. There was a row of family photographs on the mantlepiece, three girls at various stages of growing up until, in the last one, they stood together on a rocky hillside, dresses blowing in the breeze, bright smiles in the bright sunshine. They all had the same wild hair, the same freckles. Fiona and her sisters, before the war, before the bomb that shattered a family. Pulling off her woollen hat and sweeping away the red curls that tumbled around her face, Fiona indicated two chairs and we sat down, facing each other across the rag rug by the hearth.

'Would you like some tea?'

'No, not for me.'

'Something stronger?'

'No. Nothing, thank you.'

She gave me a searching look, not without humour.

'Will I need a dram after this talk?'

'It's possible, yes.' I tried for my most reassuring tone of voice. 'Can I start by saying that I have every sympathy with any nation that wants independence. I'm not motivated greatly by politics. I leave that to Ivy. But it seems only right and proper to me that any country should be able to determine its own fate and governance, if that's what its citizens desire.'

Her expression went from consternation to surprise and settled finally on wary approval.

'Why are you telling me this?'

'Because I've pieced together a story and I think you can confirm it.'

'Is that right?'

'Of course, there's no reason you should. You hardly know me and my being here is a colossal cheek, I'm well aware of that. But I'm going to ask anyway, if you'll listen.'

There was caution in her eyes but she leant back in her chair and gave me the nod to carry on. I launched in.

'In my story, a group of students from Glasgow University steal the Stone of Destiny from Westminster Abbey in the early hours of Christmas morning. One of them, a young woman, drives it north to Scotland, alone on the dark roads. How long does it take to get from London to the border? At least twelve hours, surely. By that time, she is in dire need of a break from the journey. She needs to eat and sleep before she can carry on to her final destination.' I paused and smiled. 'How am I doing?'

'It's a fine yarn.'

'I'm glad you think so. Fortunately, the young woman in my story has a friend, sympathetic to her cause, who lives in a remote spot a short detour from her route. She decides to throw herself on her friend's mercy and arrives at her door in the late afternoon of Christmas Day. How could she know that, for the first Christmas in years, the lonely house would be full of guests, and that one of them, should he discover the secret, would be a great danger to all concerned?'

I saw fear creep into Fiona's face.

'We didn't kill anyone,' she said sharply.

'We?'

'I mean me. I didn't kill anyone.'

I shook my head.

'No,' I said quietly. 'I think you meant you and your friend. She was here, wasn't she?'

Fiona's laughing eyes were deadly serious now.

'Let's be clear here, Dame Elspeth. Are you accusing me of conspiracy to steal the Stone of Destiny, of murdering Mr Coyle or both?'

'None of the above, my dear. I believe you helped a friend and a cause you believe in. That's all.'

'If that's true, why on earth would I tell you?'

'That's fair. But I'm rather fond of my own cleverness and am desperate to know if I'm right. Won't you indulge me?'

I held her gaze, watching her struggle between reticence and defiance.

'It's quite safe,' I urged. 'I give you my word that, with the exception of Ivy, I won't tell a soul about this conversation unless you give me permission to speak.'

In the end, her passion won.

'Yes. You're right. She was here and I was proud to help.'

Jubilate! as Angela Brazil loved to say. I felt a glow of triumph and beamed at her.

'How thrilling!'

'It isn't a game.' Her bright eyes flashed at me. 'Scotland has been too complacent for too long. Well, now it's had a wake-up call.'

'It certainly has. Forgive me. I'm not making fun of you. I think it's admirable.'

'Really?'

'Yes. Passion and principle should always be applauded. And courage. It was brave of them to steal the Stone.'

154

'It wasn't stolen; it was recovered.'

'Of course. Will you tell me more? I'm horribly curious. Did you know they were going to do it?'

'No.'

'Are they all your friends? Are they all at the University? How many were in on it?'

'I know them. They are decent, serious people. But the first I knew of the plan was on the wireless. Then Kay turned up on our doorstep, worn out and frozen. We put her in my bed with a hot water bottle during dinner. Then we fed her and waved her off up north.'

'We? Your parents helped?'

She hesitated, caution in her face.

'It was all my doing,' was all she said.

I understood her motives and didn't press her.

'So the Stone of Destiny was sitting outside in a car all the time that we were eating turkey and Christmas pudding?' I couldn't help myself. I laughed out loud. 'What joy!'

Fiona smiled at my delight.

'Not all of it.'

'What?'

Her eyes twinkled with mischief. 'It broke in two when they pulled it free of the chair.'

'No!'

'The boys took the big part. Kay had the small one. The police have no idea they're looking for two stones now.'

'Extraordinary! Can it be mended?'

'Eventually. When the fuss dies down. There are plenty of stone masons with an eye to an independent Scotland.'

'What a story,' I said. 'Thank you for sharing it. Thank you for trusting me.'

'To tell you true, I'm regretting it already. But what's done is done. The next move is up to you.'

'I told you. I won't give you away.'

I'm not sure that she believed me. Her freckled face was serious again.

'It has nothing to do with the murder,' she said. 'Max Coyle never came into it.'

'What time did she leave?'

'About 2am.'

'That fits. Godfrey heard her drive away.'

'When Max Coyle was still alive,' she insisted.

'It isn't quite so clear cut, though, is it? He might have seen something. Approached you afterwards. Threatened to expose you.'

'He didn't.'

'Quite a coincidence that he was killed on the same night.'

'I can't explain that.' She got to her feet, clearly signalling that it was time for me to go. 'I've been truthful with you, Dame Elspeth. I've nothing more to say now.'

I had a strong suspicion there was something she was keeping back, but I could see it was no use pressing for it. She had already answered what I had no right to ask and I told myself I had to be satisfied. It was my cue to withdraw graciously.

'My friends call me Holly,' I said, 'and I would like to count you among them, if that's all right with you?'

She looked surprised but nodded her consent with a quick smile.

156

'Holly it is, then.'

She led me out of the cosy little room and opened the front door. The cold air rushed in. Before stepping out into the snow, I turned back.

'I hope you win your fight, Fiona.'

'Oh we will,' she said with calm certainty. 'One day, I promise you, we will.'

27

In his chair by the dining room windows, Godfrey Clifford gazed out at the frozen landscape, the coffee on the table beside him cold in the cup. Again and again he went over the early hours of Boxing Day morning. What had happened, what he knew, what he couldn't explain. The events since had bewildered and shaken him. They didn't make sense at all.

A new level of threat was hanging over the snowbound house; he could feel it in the air, see it in the faces around him and he was profoundly uneasy. He wasn't afraid. Two wars had taught him what fear was, but it had no grip on him now. He was an old man. Whatever his future held, it would be a short one; he had made his peace with that. But his conscience was troubling him, the responsibility he felt for his hosts and his friends. Was his silence right or wrong? He had expected matters 'to come to a head before now, but the weather had created an unnatural hiatus. They were trapped together in this house of secrets. Would speaking out make things better or worse?

28

IVY

I took Holly's advice and had a cry, lying on my bed like I did for days when Sam died. It wasn't the same grief as then – I didn't feel numb and hopeless, I felt betrayed and angry. I was fearful, too, of what Ben might have done, what that would make him, and what it said about me that I hadn't seen it.

His words went round and round in my head. What did he think I needed protecting from? What was his big mistake? Was it me? Or was it murder? In spite of everything, I struggled to believe he could kill Max in cold blood, but how could I be sure? I didn't know him at all.

The truth was, I hadn't realised how lonely I was till Ben came along. I liked my life, my job, my friends. I felt useful and valued. Any thoughts I had about the future usually featured a vague idea of a man and maybe a family, but nothing clearer than that and I had no pressing need for either. Until I went with Holly to see Ben's play and I loved it, what he had to say and how powerfully he said it. I felt a connection with him before we ever met. Then at the first night party, there he was, quiet and unassuming amid all the glitz, and we sat in a corner and talked and laughed and a little crack opened in my ten-year-old shell.

I got up at last and washed my face. Time to get a grip, Ivy. If Ben didn't do it, the only way to know for sure was to find out who did. The lovely little butterflies of expectation I'd been carrying inside were gone and I missed them, but I still had a job to do. What doesn't kill you makes you strong, as my nan used to say. She had a platitude for every occasion.

By the time Holly came to find me, I was ready to carry on and we installed ourselves in her room to to eat the last precious chocolate limes and catch up. She looked like the cat that had got the cream and it made me smile in spite of everything.

'That's good to see,' she said. 'Brave girl.'

I didn't feel brave at all, but I wasn't up to talking about it, so I let it pass.

'I'll live. Now, come on. What are you bursting to tell me?'

'That I have been extremely clever and I have huge news.'

'You know who did it?'

'Not that clever.'

'Get on with it, then.'

She flashed me a triumphant smile and told her tale. It was much embellished and took a few frustrating detours but she got through it in the end. She sat back and looked to me for the required reaction. I stared at her in astonishment and delight and she laughed.

'The Stone of Destiny, darling. Well, a piece of it. Sitting in a Ford Anglia in the grounds of Black Gairy.'

'Bloody hell. Imagine what Andrew and Esme would say if they knew.'

'It came and went and we didn't get so much as a peek at it. But it was here.'

'Donald and Jean didn't bat an eyelid when we talked about independence,' I said.

'Seems they have a better deadpan than Fiona.'

'I believe it's true that it's her cause, not theirs. But there's nothing they wouldn't do for their girl.'

The smile died off my face.

'Does that include murder, do you reckon?'

'I don't rule it out. I don't think we can.'

'You're right. I dread to think what Max would have done with the story if he knew.'

'And he was out on the patio at the crucial time.'

I looked at her in dismay. I really liked the MacRaes. I didn't want it to be them.

'Sleuthing takes lumps out of you, doesn't it?'

'Yes, darling. Do you want to stop?'

I thought about it. Just stepping back, leaving it to time and the weather and the police. It was tempting but it was never going to happen. I don't know what it was in me, in both of us, but we wouldn't let it go. We couldn't.

'No,' I told her. 'Onward and upward.'

'That's the spirit. So what now?'

'Let's take stock. What do we know and what don't we know?'

'Have you got a prime suspect? I have.'

Not Ben, I thought. *Please, not Ben.*

'Who?'

'Sonya. It's the obvious choice.'

'I don't know. I think I believe her denial.'

'She's a fine actress, don't forget.'

'I know.' I grimaced. 'Bugger it.'

Holly unwrapped a chocolate lime and popped it in her mouth with a sigh of pleasure. 'How did we manage without these for so long?'

'War is hell.'

'Funny girl. So who do you favour, then? Still Ben?'

His face rose before my eyes. The last look he gave me before I left him. I shook it away.

'He won't explain himself,' I said.

'But he told you he didn't do it.'

'Well, he would, wouldn't he?'

'But would he kill Max because of politics?'

Holly has come a long way since we met, in terms of seeing the world from a different perspective. She never had any reason to question the status quo because it did very well by her, thank you. But she has a good heart and a generous spirit and she understands, for the most part, and when she doesn't, she humours me. There are limits though. Unlike me, she could never really understand what drives someone like Ben.

'He has passionate views about the world and Max was everything he hates. He thinks fascism could rise again and that men like Coyle make it more likely. Maybe he saw a chance to put an end to the man's malign influence and decided to take it.'

'For the greater good?'

'He's an idealist.'

I was relieved to see that she was doubtful. I wanted to be wrong. I wanted that very much.

'I think there are stronger motives in play, darling. A woman scorned, others harassed and threatened, a sensational theft to cover up. And secrets, so many secrets. Fiona is still hiding something. And Ishbel. And what wouldn't Elliot tell you?' She looked pained. 'I was so pleased with myself over the Stone business, but really, I think we've barely scratched the surface.'

The long Scottish twilight had settled in while we talked and the view through the window was mottled with mauve shadows under the darkening sky. Twenty-four hours since we stood around Max's body in the snow, since time had slowed down, and left us all in this sealed bubble of uncertainty and suspicion. I felt like the air had left my lungs then and I wouldn't take another proper breath until I knew the truth.

'You need to tackle Elliot,' I said. 'You might have more luck than I did.'

'Right. That's the next step.'

'I might have another go at Ishbel.'

'Yes. Stone or no Stone, there's still a mystery surrounding the absent Jack.'

I thought of the Stone of Destiny again, picturing Fiona's friends in the shadowy Abbey, pulling it free from the Coronation chair. How must they have felt when it came away in two pieces? Was it a curse or a blessing?

'Bit of a scoop to know it broke in half, eh?'

'And the authorities have no idea.' Holly laughed. 'The whole thing is extraordinary, isn't it?'

'Country house Christmas, you said. What a lovely time we'll have.'

'How could I possibly know...?'

'It might even snow, you said.'

'Stop it.'

'Just do me one favour?'

'What's that, darling?'

'Next time you issue a festive invitation, remind me to refuse it.'

29

Andrew Fergusson stood in the bay window of his bedroom and looked out at the night sky, bright with stars. In the moonlight, Loch Trool glistened beyond the trees and the hills behind it loomed huge and dark as sleeping giants. He thought how the people of this land had turned their eyes to this same view through the centuries, the unchanged and enduring beauty of it, and how lucky he was and how grateful for his extraordinary good fortune.

He had led a charmed life, worked for nothing and been gifted everything. Then, when Madeleine died, he had believed that life was over, in any meaningful sense. He would raise his daughter, he would pass his days in the ease his wealth bestowed and he would not expect to be happy.

And then he saw Esme Arden in a spotlight on a West End stage and everything changed. She performed the impossible, made the world whole again and brought him an excess of joy.

Was that why he had done it? To pay something back? To make a difference? To thank the stars? He had acted purely on impulse, without a thought for the consequences. It was an enormous risk. But, given the time over, he knew he would do it again. He had no defence and no regrets.

30

HOLLY

Dinner was appropriately informal. The MacRaes weren't there but Jean had produced great vats of game stew, piles of roast potatoes and buttery peas and we helped ourselves. I decided on a modest maroon two-piece, suitably sober, and observed that everyone else was dressing down as well. The mood was still solemn, but it improved with the consumption of wine, a delicious burgundy which disappeared at a rate of knots. Andrew's cellar was taking a serious hit this Christmas, but he seemed unconcerned, passing bottle after bottle around the table, alert to every drained glass; a generous, attentive host. As was Esme, at his side, keeping the conversation going, drawing everyone in, dispensing her special brand of warmth and comfort. The threat to her from Max had been eclipsed by his murder within her beloved walls but she soldiered on like a trooper nonetheless.

'I think the weather's turning.' Esme helped herself to more stew. Clearly her appetite had recovered. 'It hasn't snowed properly for hours.'

'I felt a change this afternoon,' I said. 'I think we've seen the worst of it.'

'Is the phone back on?' asked Dorothy.

'Not yet.' Andrew gave her a reassuring smile. 'It won't be much longer though, I'm sure.'

'I just wondered.'

'When are you due back on set?'

'Not till after New Year.'

'Please, God,' Elliot raised his eyes to the ceiling, 'even these roads must be clear by then.'

He went to the window and drew back the heavy drapes. Outside, the hills were ghostly in the moonlight but no snow was falling and the air was still. The sky was clear and bright with stars.

'Beautiful.' I turned to Andrew. 'So lovely.'

'You haven't seen our skies in all their glory,' he smiled. 'Some nights, you can see the Milky Way.'

'I'd be happier to see a snow plough.' Elliot returned to his seat and drained his glass.

I glared at him. He had dissipated the fragile peace in the room. I could see it in the faces around me. Ivy was looking anywhere but at Ben, who was pushing his food around his plate, deep in his own thoughts. Godfrey was staring at everyone in turn, his eyes full of questions. Ishbel reached out to squeeze her father's hand and he responded in kind. Esme gathered herself, but it was Sonya who drew focus. Instead of skirting round the elephant in the room, she met it head on.

'Snow or no snow, we aren't going anywhere for a good while yet. The police will come and they won't want anyone leaving till they know what happened. Until they make an arrest.'

All eyes turned. I could almost hear their thoughts. Which one of us? Who is it?

Sonya looked from face to face with a dark smile.

'You guys still have capital punishment, right?'

'Sonya!' Esme's voice was sharp.

'Just a thought.'

'Not helpful.'

'Pardon me for wondering if whoever knifed my husband will swing for it. Jesus, the English are hilarious! Murder is fine and dandy but God forbid we should be impolite about it.'

Andrew got to his feet.

'I'm ready for an armchair and a coffee if anyone wants to join me.'

He offered Esme an arm and she took it. They walked through the double doors to the drawing room, Ishbel with them. Ben stood up and followed, walking past Ivy without a look. I saw her hands clench in her lap and felt her misery.

Sonya looked around at us defiantly.

'Ok, ok. It was mean. But I'm right, aren't I?'

'Sonya, darling.' I pushed my plate aside. 'I know all this is awful and so much worse for you. I never mind you being rude, but I mind you being cruel. Go and make your peace with our lovely hosts. You all deserve that.'

She gave me a hard stare and then shrugged her shoulders and flashed me a smile. 'You win. I'll play nice.'

She threw down her napkin and followed them. There was a general air of relief as the door closed behind her.

'Well done.' Godfrey patted my hand and rose from his seat.

'Are you going in for act two?' asked Elliot. 'I admire your stamina.'

'Actually, I'm going to my room. I'm rather tired tonight.'

'Can I bring you anything?' Ivy asked him but he shook his head.

'Thank you, no.'

This horrible business was taking its toll on him. On all of us, of course, but Godfrey was well into his eighties and the strain was showing. He was leaning heavily on his cane as he went out.

'Poor Godfrey,' said Dorothy. 'He looks worn out.'

'Aren't we all, darling?'

Elliot reached for the wine bottle and poured himself another ample glass. He was in one of his acid moods but I damped down my irritation because I could see that beneath his louche exterior, he was strung tight. Something was eating away at him and I meant to find out what it was. I gave Ivy a meaningful look and she took the hint.

'Come on,' she said to Dorothy. 'Let's give the gramophone a whirl.'

They headed for the library, leaving Elliot and I alone at the table.

'And then there were two,' he said. 'Will you stay and drink with me?'

It was exactly the invitation I wanted.

'Of course, darling. But there's a price. You have to tell me what I want to know.'

'And that would be?'

'What Max Coyle did to hurt you so badly.'

He closed up like an oyster shell.

'No deal, my dear. Leave if you must.'

'Was he threatening you?' I persisted.

'Of course he was.' He gave me a bitter smile. 'My sex life is illegal. A man like Coyle would never let an opportunity like that go to waste.'

That part of the story was shared without a qualm. What more was there? What was he afraid of? Ashamed of?

'So he was holding something over you. He made a habit of that, it seems. But what did he want from you in return?'

His face was frozen but his eyes were burning as he emptied his glass and filled it again. The intensity of his loathing came across the table in waves. It was easy to believe that it could lead to murder and I was horribly afraid that it had.

'I didn't kill him.' Elliot knew what I was thinking. 'I might despise myself less if I had.'

'Why do you say that?' When he didn't answer, I persevered. 'Whatever it is, you need to share it. For your own sake. It's eating you up.'

I could see that my words had reached him, through the haze of wine and the accumulated tension of the last few days. He sagged in his seat, looking unutterably weary, as the resistance left him. My heart went out to him and I reached for his hand. He was trembling.

'Information,' he said simply. 'That was Max Coyle's currency.'

'Of course.'

'He got his hands on a letter I wrote. A foolish, unguarded letter. Enough to ruin me.'

'And he blackmailed you?'

He nodded. 'For years. I gave him names, told him who to follow, where to send photographers.'

'The man was a vampire.'

He looked up at me with a curl of his lips and the faintest hint of his usual sardonic self in his eyes.

'I stole his briefcase today.'

'What?'

'I took it from his bedroom. Broke it open. I hoped the letter would be in it. But it wasn't there. He's dead but it's still hanging over me. I'm still in danger.'

'Oh, Elliot, I'm so sorry.'

The life went out of him again. 'Don't waste your sympathy on me, darling. I'm not worth it.'

'I don't believe that.'

'You haven't heard the worst.' He was gripping my hand so tightly it hurt. Silent tears welled in his eyes. When he spoke again, it was little more than a whisper. 'Miles. Miles Darnley.'

My heart lurched and I barely stifled a gasp. A young actor, Miles Darnley, had approached a man in a public lavatory who turned out to be an undercover policeman. The trial was sensationalised in Coyle's papers with headlines about plagues of sodomy and moral rot in the artistic community. A sweet, talented boy who fell from matinee idol to pariah, Miles served six months in jail and gassed himself in his flat a week after his release.

'Oh. Elliot.'

'I gave his name.' He dropped my hand as if it was red hot. 'You hate me now.'

'No.'

'You should. I hate myself.'

'I hate unjust laws. I hate bigots and the monsters that feed them.'

'I'm a coward. I sold out my friends to save myself.'

He waited, watching my face. I couldn't lie to him. I owed him more than that.

'Yes,' I said quietly. 'You did.'

'Would you have done it?'

I looked deep inside myself before answering.

'I hope not,' I said. 'But I don't know.'

He put his head in his hands and wept and I walked round the table and wrapped my arms about him. I told myself I was glad that Max Coyle was dead and then I felt ashamed and heavy with sadness at man's inhumanity to man. I knew Elliot's secret now and with all my heart I wished that I didn't.

31

IVY

'It's a strong motive.'

'Yes. And more than that, he has lost faith in himself, in his ability to do the right thing. That must make it easier to do the wrong thing, mustn't it?'

'Poor Elliot,' I whispered.

'It was awful, darling. He was broken. I stayed with him till he calmed down, took him to his room and tucked him in, but I doubt he slept much.'

Holly was sitting on the edge of my bed. She had woken me up at the crack of doom, impatient to share the news. It was still dark outside and we talked in the glow from my bedside lamp, a bright patch of light in the shadowy room. She was wearing the shawl I'd bought her for Christmas over her silk pyjamas, holding it around herself, as if it was more for comfort than warmth.

'You look tired out yourself,' I said.

'I'm fine darling.'

'I've never known you have so many early mornings.'

'What about when we're filming and up with the lark?'

'True enough.'

'Though I admit, filming is less emotionally wearing than murder.'

I patted her arm. 'Shall I make us a cup of tea?'

The British answer to everything. She gave me a little smile.

'Yes, please. Shall we go through to mine?'

We took up our usual places, drank our tea and ate some biscuits as the morning light seeped into the sky.

'Dawn does seem to be getting a habit with us. Who'd have thought it?'

'It will all change when my next play opens. Back to theatre rules.'

I'd had to learn, when I started working for her, that theatre people have their own timetable, shifted round a few hours from the usual. Curtain down at ten or so, a bite of supper, a bit of time to wind down and bed at two in the morning is the routine – later, if there's an after-show party or whatever. If you like your eight hours, like Holly does, that's your morning gone for a Burton. Breakfast is often at midday.

I was looking at the view, at the silver line of the loch shining beyond the trees.

'London seems a long way away, doesn't it?'

'A different universe. I feel like we've lived a lifetime since we got here.'

'It can't be much longer. The weather has definitely changed and the roads will be passable soon.'

Holly looked at me over her teacup, her eyes as blue as a Mediterranean sky. Even in the unforgiving sunlight and free of make-up, she still looked ten years younger than her age.

'We've got a murderer to catch before then.'

I thought of Ben, hiding himself from me, of Elliot's pain

and Fiona's passion, of the misery Max Coyle manufactured and profited from.

'Does it really matter?'

'I know what you mean.' Her smile was sympathetic. 'But it does matter, my darling. It must or we're all lost.'

She was right, of course. She usually was. We had to keep digging, even if we didn't like what we found.

I felt hemmed in and the early morning world outside called to me. A wander in the crisp air to blow away the cobwebs. Holly was far from keen. Her armchair was cosy and comfortable and there was still tea in the pot.

'Really? Before breakfast?'

'The best time.'

'Don't be hearty. It doesn't suit you.'

But she gave way in the end and shooed me off to get dressed. When I came back, she was ready in coat, scarf, hat and gloves.

'I have no sensible shoes,' she said mournfully. 'It will have to be boots from the cloakroom.'

We went downstairs, selected a pair each and headed out. Holly winced as the cold air hit us.

'A short walk,' she said firmly.

'Chin up. It's lovely.'

It really was. The stained-glass panels of the front door were shooting colours onto the porch steps and the sandstone walls sparkled in the morning sunlight. From the garden, I turned and looked back at the house, standing serene in its timeless landscape, solid and permanent. It would still be there when we were all long gone. I was comforted by the thought.

Crunching through the frozen snow, we wandered into the trees.

'It's like a scene from the *Snow Queen*,' said Holly, who was cheering up a bit. 'Have you read that new book about an icy kingdom on the other side of a cupboard? What's it called?'

'The kingdom or the book?'

'Both, please.'

'Narnia. *The Lion, the Witch and the Wardrobe.*'

'Ah, yes. Wardrobe not cupboard. You have read it?'

'I gave it to my niece for Christmas but had a quick look before I bought it, in case it was too preachy. It's by C.S. Lewis. Remember those broadcasts he did during the war?'

'Vaguely.'

'Some of them were interesting, even for godless heathens like me. He touched on philosophy and physics, all kinds of stuff, but essentially they were about his faith. He's devout. So I thought the book might be too religious for my liking. But I didn't need to worry. The symbolism is pretty heavy but there's a lot more to it. It's fun.'

Holly looked at me as I prattled on and, when I was done, she laughed.

'You're such an intellectual.'

'Behave.'

'You should be holed up at Girton or Sommerville, publishing papers and wafting about in a cap and gown.'

'I think working-class girls from Morecambe are a bit thin on the ground at Oxbridge.'

'Well, that's their loss.' She smiled. 'And my gain.'

The smile was wiped from her face as she looked back at the house. 'Oh dear. Here comes trouble.'

I turned and my heart flipped in my chest. Ben was coming towards us. My first instinct was to walk away. Our last encounter had been awful and I couldn't face more of the same. But as I moved, he called out.

'Ivy. Wait!'

'Shall I go, darling?' Holly asked.

I shook my head. I didn't want to be alone with him. As he drew closer, I saw the strain in his face and it tugged at my heart but I hardened myself against him. He had a lot of explaining to do.

Coming to a standstill, he looked from me to Holly. What he saw wasn't encouraging. She had a face like stone. But he persevered.

'I saw you from the house.'

'And?'

'Can we talk?'

'What's the point?'

'We can't leave things like this.'

'Then tell me the truth.'

'Ivy, darling,' Holly said quietly, 'I feel like the spectre at the feast. Please give me leave to depart.'

'I'd rather you didn't.'

'This is between the two of you. Hear him out, at least.'

Ben's eyes were pleading with me and I caved in, like the fool I am.

'All right. You win.'

Holly squeezed my arm and walked away.

'Make it right, Ben,' she said to him as she passed. 'I don't think you'll get another chance and you won't deserve one.'

Something whizzed past my shoulder. There was a loud crack, then another and another. Tree bark scattered like shrapnel in the air around us.

'What...?'

I didn't get to finish my question. Ben dived for me, throwing me to the ground.

'Get down!' he yelled to Holly as he covered my body with his. I saw her flatten herself against the snow as Ben's weight knocked the breath out of me. 'Are you all right?' he asked. 'Are you hit?'

'What in the name of...?' Holly's voice was shrill.

'Ivy? Talk to me.'

'I'm fine.' I fought for air. 'Was that a gun?'

'What about you Holly?' he called over his shoulder.

'Unscathed. Can we get up?'

'No. Don't move.'

'But it's stopped. Hasn't it?'

'Stay where you are!' He rolled off me and I sucked in cold air, fighting for breath. He was still using his body to shield me as he looked around us. 'They might be waiting to take another shot.'

'So it wasn't an accident?' I gasped. 'They were aiming at us?'

I was shaking like a leaf. Ben took my face in his hands and let out a long breath of relief.

'I thought you were hit.'

Whatever else was going on, what I saw in his eyes put an end to any doubts I had about his feelings for me. A nugget of happiness lodged itself in my chest, glowing warm despite the fear and the freezing cold seeping through my clothes. I held onto it, lying there on my back, looking at the winter sky above the tops of the trees, listening intently for any sound, but there was nothing but silence and stillness, as if the last few minutes had never happened. My heart thudding in my chest told me otherwise.

After a few minutes that seemed like hours, Ben made a move.

'All right. Let's chance it. Keep away from open ground. Stay in the trees.'

He went to give Holly a hand up as I got to my feet. My every nerve was tensed for another shot ringing out, but nothing happened and I started to breathe easier as we headed deeper into the trees, taking the long route back to the house.

'What on earth just happened?' Holly's eyes were wide with shock. 'I can barely believe it.'

'Someone tried to shoot us.' I couldn't stop the wobble in my voice.

Ben came to a halt, an unreadable expression on his face.

'It was meant for me.'

'What? Why?'

'I could have got you both killed. I'm so sorry.'

Holly's face filled with cold fury. 'Now listen to me, young man. My patience with you and whatever you are hiding from us is utterly exhausted—'

If I knew Holly, there was a lot more where that came from, but Ben got a lucky escape. A cry rang out and Andrew came running through the trees with Esme in his wake.

'We heard shots.'

'Are you hurt?' Esme asked.

Holly's gaze was still fixed on Ben. 'This conversation isn't over.'

She turned to the new arrivals. 'No casualties, except for some shaken nerves. But someone was using us for target practice.'

'Oh God.' Esme gathered me and Holly in a bear hug.

'It was rifle fire,' Ben said to Andrew. 'You have guns here, I suppose?'

'For hunting. There's a gun cupboard in my study.'

'Locked?'

'Not always.' Andrew grimaced. 'Not when it's only adults in the house.'

'This is a nightmare!' Esme was near to tears. 'What next? Is no one safe?'

She was right. The situation had taken a new turn. An isolated crime of passion was one thing, but someone prepared to kill any and all of us was quite another.

'Where did the shots come from?' Andrew was scanning the grounds as he spoke.

I shook my head. The whole thing was a bit of a blur and I had no idea.

'Not the foggiest, darling,' said Holly.

'Behind the summer house, at a guess.' Ben looked up to our left and I remembered he was more used to being shot at than we were. 'Shall we all get indoors, to be on the safe side?'

Andrew nodded and ushered us all towards the house. Esme clung to me and Holly like she'd never let go. I studied Ben's expression as we walked, trying to read his thoughts, but had no luck. Why did he believe the shots were aimed at him?

Presumably he knew who fired them. Was that the same person who murdered Max? It would seem likely. So it wasn't Ben? That was good news. But why shoot at him?

I felt like my brain would explode. I had to get the full story from Ben. However bad it was, it would be better than the agony of not knowing. As soon as I could get him away from the crowd, I'd carry on where Holly left off and make him tell me. But as we approached the side of the house, Andrew said something to him and the two of them broke away.

'You go in,' Ben said to the three of us. 'We won't be long.'

'What are you doing?'

'Just checking.'

'The summer house?' Esme's voice was fearful. 'Be careful!'

I watched them climb the slope and disappear into the trees, my ears straining for any sound, willing them to come back, but there was nothing to hear or see.

'Come on, darling.' Holly took my elbow and led me across the patio. 'Early or no, I need a stiff drink.'

The French windows to the dining room were standing open. Ishbel was there with Godfrey, his face creased with concern.

'What happened?' he asked as soon as we were within hearing distance.

Esme laid a hand on his shoulder. 'No one hurt,' she said.

'It was gunfire?'

'Yes.'

'I don't understand what's happening.' Godfrey shook his head, bewilderment in his face. 'I feel I'm going mad.'

'I know what you mean,' I said heavily.

'We were eating breakfast,' said Ishbel. 'The three of us. Godfrey had just arrived. Then we heard...' She broke off in disbelief.

'But who...?' asked Godfrey, almost in a whisper. 'And why?'

Esme crouched by his chair and took his hand, but he didn't look at her. His gaze was fixed outside.

'Where is Andrew?' he asked.

'At the summer house, with Ben. They think the shots were fired from there.'

'Here they come now,' said Holly.

They were picking their way down, two dark figures against the silver sky. Andrew was carrying something. As they came closer, I saw it was a rifle and a shiver ran through me like a trickle of ice water.

'It was just lying there in the snow,' he said as they came into the room. 'Whoever fired at you dropped it and ran.'

'Lock it away, Andrew.' Esme shuddered. 'I know it's closing the stable door after the horse has bolted but I can't bear to look at it.'

He strode away to his study on the other side of the hall. Holly crossed to the sideboard and poured generous measures of whisky from the decanter, taking a gulp of her own before handing round the rest. A shocked silence descended. Ishbel sat at the table. Ben stood with his back to the room, staring out of the window. Godfrey was motionless in his chair, his face haggard. I realised my legs were shaking and knocked back my drink in the hope it would steady me. When Andrew came back in, he gathered Esme to him, kissing the top of her head. I felt he was holding her upright, that she would sink to the floor if he let go.

'Do you think the others heard the shots?' she asked him.

'It seems not.'

'Should we tell them what happened?'

'I don't think we can keep it from them, darling. There's someone in this house who is a danger to us all. Early tomorrow, I'm going to walk to Newton Stewart and fetch the police. We can't leave it any longer. Meantime, we should all be on our guard.'

'How are you now?' She looked across at the three of us.

'I'm wet through and freezing,' said Holly. 'I need a hot bath.'

'You should all do that. We'll save breakfast for you.' In spite of everything, Esme was still Esme.

'Bless you, darling. And don't worry. We're all fine.'

Speak for yourself, I thought, but I didn't say it. Holly bundled Ben and me into the hall and up the stairs. On the landing, she paused and turned to him.

'Come to my room when you're ready and we'll pick up where we left off.'

That couldn't happen soon enough for me. But nothing is simple, is it? Ben gave me a look that was part sorrow, part defiance and my heart sank. I knew what he was going to say.

'I'm sorry. Things have changed. I can't talk to you now.'

'But—' Holly stared at him in disbelief.

'Ben.' I put out my hand, but he stepped away, avoiding my eyes.

'It's no use.' There was resignation in his voice. 'If you believe I killed Max, I can't stop you. I wouldn't blame you.'

'I don't understand.'

'I'm sorry.'

He walked away and climbed the stairs to the next floor. I watched him till he was out of sight but he didn't look back. At my side, Holly spluttered with frustration.

'The man speaks in riddles!'

Suddenly I was weary to the bone. There was so much to think about, but my mind was numb. I wanted to sink into warm water and never get out.

Holly took one look at my face, hooked her arm through my arm, led me to the bathroom and turned on the taps.

'You first,' she said.

'Thank you.'

'Soak it all away.' She poured out bath salts from an ornate bottle. They smelt like heaven. 'It's been quite a morning.'

'Hasn't it?'

'This too will pass, darling. All will be well.'

She gave me a hug and left me to it. I shed my wet clothes, lay down in the bath, closed my eyes and tried very hard to believe her.

32

Fiona MacRae closed her book and added it to the pile on her bedside table. The intricacies of corporate law struggled to hold her attention at the best of times. Today it didn't stand a chance. She was on edge, desperate for news of her friends and the Stone. Had Kay made it to her family croft through the worsening weather? What had happened to the other piece? Where were the boys? How close had the police come to the truth? Would they be knocking on the lodge door any time soon? When would the weather break? Fiona thought she would run mad with unanswered questions.

She jumped to her feet and went to the window. Opening the top pane, she stood looking out, enjoying the tingle of cold air on her face. The white world outside was still and quiet, the trees unmoving and heavy with snow. This is where she had stood on the night of the murder, too full of adrenaline to sleep. The anxiety in her freckled face deepened. She had more than the Stone of Destiny to worry about. Protecting people was one thing but where should her loyalties lie? Was that her decision to make? Just how long could she keep to herself what she had seen?

33

HOLLY

Poor Ivy looked at the end of her tether and who could blame her. Mystery piling on mystery, a brush with death and, on top of everything else, a thorny love affair to deal with. What, for the love of god, was Ben playing at? I wanted to shake him till he rattled.

I got into my robe, wrapped my shawl around me and dropped into my favourite chair as I waited for my turn in the bath. The morning's events were replaying like a film reel in my head, the sharp crack of the gun fire still echoing in my ears. I shivered and not from cold. Was Ben right? Were the bullets meant for him? I closed my eyes and tried to settle my thoughts into some kind of order.

He had been going to tell us what his trouble was, but the shooting changed his mind. If he knew something about the murder, he might believe it was an attempt to silence him. In that case, telling us would put us in the same danger. So he was protecting us? Whoever the target was, the fact that he was shot at too meant that he couldn't be the killer, didn't it? That was something for Ivy to hold onto, at least.

I could guess at the scenarios playing in her head. Everyone tortures themselves trying to picture what we can never know but need to see. When Tom died, I had no idea what the anodyne words 'Killed in Action' were hiding from me, so I constructed detailed tableaux in my mind, agonising scenes of mutilation, of blood and rats and mud. I lay awake through long nights, shaking with horror at my own imaginings. It was irrational and it was hell, but it was inevitable. As the great bard said, 'reason and love keep little company together'. We needed to solve this mystery once and for all, because Ivy would be tormenting herself every waking hour until we did.

I was relieved to see she looked better when she came in, still flushed from the bath and in the red sweater that suited her so well.

'Sorry it took so long. I've run yours for you.'

'Thank you, darling.'

'What's that?'

She pointed. There was a folded sheet of paper on the floor by the door.

'Has that been there all the time? I missed it.'

'You came in through the bathroom.'

'Of course.' I retrieved it and opened it up. There was a short message in capital letters. I read it out loud. '*Take the warning. Back off.*'

Ivy's eyes widened. 'Bloody hell.'

'Bloody hell indeed.'

'So Ben was wrong. The bullets were meant for us.'

'It would seem so.'

'Can I see it?' I passed it over. 'I don't recognise the writing. Do you?'

'Disguised, I'm sure.'

Ivy was staring at the paper.

'If it was a warning, it was meant to miss us. That's some comfort, I suppose.'

'It was a huge risk. A stray bullet or a ricochet...' I shuddered. 'Someone is worryingly irresponsible.'

'Or desperate.'

'I suppose it means we're on the right track.' I looked at her closely. She had looked utterly defeated standing on the landing, watching Ben walk away. 'Do you still want to do this?'

I absolutely couldn't stop but I wouldn't have blamed her if she wanted to. However, she answered without hesitation. 'Yes.'

'Are you sure?'

'Too bloody right I am. It's personal now.'

'Good. In that case, we need to assess where we are. Update the list.'

'First things first. You go and get your bath whilst I nip down to fetch us some breakfast.' She gave me something close to one of her old cheeky grins. 'I don't know about you but dicing with death makes me hungry as hell.'

*

'Max was here for two days before he was killed,' I said. 'Is the timing relevant, do you think?'

I was bathed and dressed and we were working our way through a mountain of bacon sandwiches whilst we talked. Esme had given Ivy a tray to bring upstairs and tailored the contents to her own appetite, by the looks of it. Still, we were doing it justice. It seemed like a week since last night's dinner.

'I don't think it was planned,' Ivy said. 'I think it was a spur of the moment thing, a crime of passion. You don't stick a dagger in someone's neck unless you're white hot with emotion, do you?'

'That's what I'm getting at. Did something happen that night to trigger it? Something we could well have witnessed without knowing its significance.'

'That's a thought.'

'You need to do your thing again, darling. Take us through the evening.'

I settled down in my chair with another sandwich and waited expectantly.

'Well,' Ivy began, 'it started with champagne and everyone in their glad rags. Just after we arrived, Dorothy asked Andrew about his *sgian dubh*, remember? He took it from his stocking and showed it to her.'

'Oh, Lord. She asked if it was sharp.'

'It's a natural enough question, really.'

'A few hours before Max was stabbed with one?'

'Fair enough. Black mark for Dorothy.'

'Then again, it could have put the idea in someone else's mind.' I waved a hand. 'Carry on for now.'

'Yes, Your Dameship.'

'Sorry. Was I bossy?'

'No more than usual.'

'That's all right, then.'

She cast her mind back again.

'Elliot had a little dig at Ishbel. About Jack. But Esme smoothed it over. Me and Ben stood guard over Dorothy when

Max arrived. There was some talk about his tartan and he was rude to Andrew. Then he had a little spat with Ishbel about the difference between independence and devolution.'

'He ruffled a few feathers, didn't he?'

'Always.'

'Then what?'

'Sonya arrived. She was pretty tipsy and looking for a fight.'

'Yes. She brought up the Fedorov thing. Blamed Max for that poor girl's death.'

'What girl?'

'Harry Parker.'

Ivy was reaching towards the tray for more food, but she paused with her hand outstretched and stared at me, confused.

'Harry Parker was a girl?'

'Didn't you know?'

'No idea. I'd never heard about any of it till the other night.'

'Before your time, darling.'

'Ben knew all about it.'

'He would. She's a Communist hero.'

'With a name like Harry, I just assumed it was a boy.'

'No. She was a lovely young woman. Only nineteen. It was a terrible...' I broke off, looking at the excitement dawning in her face. 'What? What is it?'

'Bloody hell. Is it that simple?' Ivy whispered.

'What?'

'A boy's name.'

'What are you talking about?'

'I think I've solved one of our mysteries.'

'For pity's sake!'

190

'Sorry. I just thought how lots of girl's names can be shortened to sound like a boy. Harriet, Georgina, Thomasina...' She paused for dramatic effect and I glared at her.

'Ivy Earnshaw, I swear—'

'Jacqueline,' she finished triumphantly.

'What?'

'Jack.'

Light dawned.

'Jack,' I repeated.

We looked at each other, smiling like idiots.

'Oh,' I breathed. 'Dear Ishbel.'

'Is that what she's hiding?'

'I believe it could be.'

The love that dare not speak its name.

'We should talk to her,' said Ivy. 'If it's true and if Max knew and threatened her with exposure—'

She didn't need to finish.

'Come on,' I said. 'Let's go and find her.'

*

Ishbel was in the kitchen, stirring soup at the range. Jean was there too, filling a basket with fresh bread rolls. True to type, there was no drama from Mrs MacRae. She nodded when she saw us but didn't pause in her work.

'You've had an exciting morning, ladies.'

'You can say that again.'

'So many times I've told the men to keep those guns locked away. They might listen now.'

191

'Too late.'

'Aye. Well, I'm glad you're both safe.'

With that, she picked up the bread and made for the door and the minute she was gone, we descended on Ishbel. Jean could be back any minute. Ivy put on her best you-can-trust-me smile and launched right in.

'Is Jack short for Jacqueline?'

The effect was dramatic. Ishbel froze on the spot, the spoon motionless, red flooding into her cheeks. She didn't need to answer. It was as clear as day. Her boyfriend was a girlfriend.

'Sorry to be so blunt.' I took the spoon from her hand and tended to the soup. 'But please don't be upset. Your secret is safe.'

'How did you know?'

'A lucky guess.'

'And it makes no difference to us. Theatre people don't care about all that.'

'Ivy's right, darling. It's everyday life for us.'

'Well, it isn't for me.' Ishbel's voice was bitter. 'Or Jack. Her family would never understand. They'd be bewildered. Devastated. And the University is no better. Two girls were sent down last term when some moral crusader reported them.'

'I'm sorry,' Ivy said. 'Bloody hell. It's 1950 not 1850. Aren't we progressing at all?'

'This is ready.' I took the pan off the heat. 'You know, my dear girl, Esme would be a tower of strength to you in all this. Why haven't you confided in her?'

'Because I can't expect her to keep it from my father and I'm too afraid to tell him.' Ishbel wiped tears away impatiently. 'We need to take this conversation elsewhere. Jean's coming back.'

'You two find a private spot,' I said. 'I'll stay and help in here.'

It was heroic of me because I was burning with curiosity but I thought Ishbel would be happier talking to someone nearer her own age. I gave her a hug, then shooed them off. They got a keen look from Jean in the doorway but she asked no questions. She waited till they were gone, then made her only comment on the situation.

'It's a house full of secrets, right enough.'

With that, she went through to the scullery, putting an end to the conversation. I presumed she was thinking of her daughter and the Stone of Destiny. But was there more she wasn't telling me? I wouldn't be surprised. Quite honestly, after the festive season at Black Gairy, I didn't think anything would ever surprise me again.

34

IVY

We tried the library and found it empty. Sitting either side of the fire, we took up where we had left off. I wouldn't have been surprised if she had stonewalled me, told me to mind my own business, but she didn't. I think it was a relief for her to tell someone at last, say the words out loud. But even then, it didn't come easy. Secrecy is a habit it can be difficult to break.

Ishbel didn't meet my eyes. There was a loose thread on her bottle-green sweater and she pulled at it as she spoke, staring down at her busy hands.

'It isn't a schoolgirl crush.'

'I understand that.'

'I tried to have relationships with men, to do the accepted thing, but it was an empty pretence. Then I met Jack and fell in love for the first time in my life.'

'You're lucky to have found each other.'

'Yes, we are.' Her fingers stilled and she raised her head at last. 'We should be able to shout it from the rooftops, but instead we sneak around as if we're ashamed. We're both terrified of our families finding out. Her people are religious. Devout.'

'Does Andrew have a faith?'

'No.' There was infinite sadness in the smile she gave me. 'But he's a conventional man. He embraces your world because he adores Esme and he has a generous spirit, but at heart he's a traditionalist. It would change how he sees me and it would break my heart to see the disappointment in his eyes.'

The tears came again and this time she let them flow. What a complicated business life is. Pain is the price we pay for love. That's why we have to wring every ounce of joy from it, fight for our happiness and hold it tight.

'I think you should trust him. He loves you a lot.'

'I've already lost one parent. I can't lose another.'

'You won't lose him.'

'How do you know that? You can't know for sure.' Her face crumpled again. 'I'm scared.'

She was right. It was easy to second guess Andrew's reaction but I couldn't be certain. It was hypocritical to dismiss her, when I was held back by fear too. Scared of not knowing but scared of the truth. I needed to practice what I preached.

When Ishbel went up to wash her face and gather herself before lunch, I climbed the stairs with her, all the way to the second floor. I decided I wouldn't wave goodbye to Ben until I'd done every single thing I could to keep him. She went into her room and I knocked on his door.

*

He was recently out of the bath and in his dressing gown, his hair still wet and tussled. He looked lovely. I chided myself for weakness and tried to get a grip but I couldn't find a word to say. We just stood on opposite sides of the doorway, staring at each other in silence. At last he took a step back and motioned me into the room, closing the door behind me. I stood in the middle of the floor with my heart hammering in my chest, in disbelief at the state I was reduced to. All of a sudden, he covered the distance between us in two strides and wrapped his arms around me. There were a hundred reasons why I should have pushed him away and made a run for the hills, but I didn't. I couldn't.

'I'm sorry,' he whispered into my hair. 'I'm so sorry.'

I could feel his breath, warm on my cheek. He smelt of soap and shaving cream.

'Ben.'

It was all I could say. His name. I was shaking. He held me tighter.

'I hate that I hurt you.'

'You have to tell me the truth.' I found my voice. 'Whatever it is.'

I raised my head and looked into his face. His heart was in his eyes.

'I can't.'

I forced myself to move out of his arms and away from him.

'So what do we do?'

'I didn't kill Max. I swear it on whatever you like to name. I did something stupid and I don't know how to make it right. But I didn't kill him. Please believe me.'

Everything in me wanted to believe him, but there were too many unknowns, too much secrecy. Suddenly weary, I sat on the end of his bed.

'What was it? The stupid thing?'

He didn't answer. He just shook his head helplessly.

'Was it wrong, what you did? Can you tell me that, at least?'

He gave me a wonky little smile. 'Depends what you mean by wrong.'

'Illegal?'

'Definitely.'

'Immoral?'

'Not in my eyes. God, this is such a mess!'

He sat beside me and took hold of my hand.

'I'm sorry. I can't say it enough. I wish I could make it all go away, but this is where we are. It's unfair of me to ask but I'm asking anyway. Please trust me. I can't lose you, Ivy. I can't.'

He was looking deep into my face, as if I was the most precious thing in the world, and there were tears in his eyes. In that moment, I forgot what we were talking about, I forgot where we were, I forgot everything but the urge to reach out for him. *I'm sorry, Sam, love*, I thought, *I'm sorry, but I've lost the fight with this man. I can't resist the pull of him any longer.*

Ben's eyes widened and his lips parted slightly. I could feel my heart pounding. I could hear myself breathing. I don't know how long we sat there. It seemed like an age and it seemed no time at all. And then we were kissing.

It was a while before we came up for air. When we did, we just stared at each other, lost for words. He brushed a curl off my face and tucked it behind my ear. I thought if I could freeze one moment for ever, it would be this one.

'I do trust you,' I said. 'I need my head reading, but I do.'

Impatiently I sought out his lips again. He moved into my

arms, pressing close and warm and everything else fell away. I sank into him without a second thought and there was nothing in the world but us.

35

'Better keep the gun cupboard locked from now on.'

Andrew had left Esme and Ishbel at the house and walked down to the lodge for a word with Donald. As he trudged through the snow, he wondered if a shot would ring out from somewhere, angry that he had to consider even the possibility in his own grounds, where he had always felt so secure. He and Esme had vowed to each other that they wouldn't let what had happened ruin Black Gairy for them and, in his heart, he believed that nothing really could. Nonetheless, he was on edge and he resented it.

Finding Donald in the shed, he handed over the spare key he had brought with him.

'It was foolish to leave it open, I suppose.'

'Aye.' Donald smiled wryly. 'Jean had a few words to say on the subject.'

'Ears still burning?'

'She's a woman of strong opinions, right enough.'

Andrew laughed.

'My grandfather used to say he'd rather face the warring clans than an irate Jean MacRae.'

'And she was only a slip of a girl in those days.' Donald shook his head. 'But still fierce.'

'Strong women, my friend. Our curse and our blessing.'

'That's right.'

'There's my Esme, still battling. A murdered guest in the summer house and assassination attempts in the garden but the show must go on.'

The humour died out of Donald's face.

'Not the Christmas she planned,' he said. 'I'm sorry for that. And does she know about the other thing?'

'No. That's between us for now.'

'Fair enough.'

They shared a moment's understanding before Andrew stirred himself.

'We have to bring the police in though, whatever the risk. It can't wait any longer.'

'I see that.'

'I'm going to Newton Stewart tomorrow.'

'I'll walk with you.'

'Into the lion's den.'

'Aye.'

Andrew nodded and smiled.

'Then I'll be glad of the company. Thank you.'

36

HOLLY

I went into lunch, though I was still stuffed to the gunnels with bacon sandwiches. I wanted a good look at the assembled company, to see if I could tell who shot at me by staring into their eyes. Of course I couldn't. Even my special powers have their limits.

My plan was hindered further by the poor turnout, with several people missing. There was no sign of Ivy but Ishbel was there, sitting between Dorothy and Elliot, joining in the small talk. She gave me a little smile when I caught her eye. No hard feelings, it seemed. I was glad of that.

Dorothy was relaxed, despite her tight-fitting dress and high heels, and she ate with a good appetite. Ivy was right that the loss of Max seemed to be a blessing for her. Should we have discounted her so quickly? Then again, I couldn't see her firing off a few rounds from a hunting rifle, no matter how hard I tried.

I moved on to Elliot, suave as ever in Hardy Amies, his hair sleek, his arch smile in place, as if his confession to me had never happened. All I got from him was a raised eyebrow and the slightest tilt of his head. No one would guess the load he was carrying. Long years of secrecy had honed the performance to perfection. Pride goeth before a fall, I told myself. My powers of perception had met their match in Elliot Mayhew.

Having said that, I could read Esme's thoughts easily enough. She was chatting to everyone in turn, still the perfect hostess, but she was paler than ever and I could see the strain behind her smile. She sat next to Sonya, who looked quietly stunning in a dark blue shift with a Hermes scarf at her neck.

That made six at table. Ivy, Godfrey, Andrew and Ben hadn't made an appearance. Esme said Godfrey was resting and she'd taken a tray to his room. Jean and Donald were absent too but towards the end of the meal, Fiona came in with cheese and biscuits. She gave me a searching look, wondering if my promise was good, I suppose, if her secret was safe. I felt weighed down by the avalanche of confidences, but I had no one to blame but myself and my poking and prying. And after all of it, was a solution any nearer? Not remotely. So many motives, so little time. I needed to talk to Ivy.

When Ishbel and I were clearing dishes and had a moment alone in the kitchen corridor, I asked her where they had parted company.

'On the top corridor. She went to Ben's room.'

That was big news. Another row or a reconciliation? I hoped it was the latter, even though it was playing with fire. But she loved him, that was as clear as day. Her happiness depended on him and Ivy's happiness was as important to me as my own, so with all my heart I wished for the two of them to find a way through.

I was the last to leave the kitchen after the lunch dishes were done, except for Fiona and Jean, who were heads together at the table. As I crossed to the door, Jean looked up and I knew I had been the subject of their hushed conversation. I gave her my most reassuring smile and her serious face softened a little.

'I hope Fiona's right to trust you, Dame Elspeth.'

'She is.'

'It said on the wireless this morning that the police have new information.'

'They don't know anything, Mum. They're dragging the Serpentine.' Fiona chuckled. 'They're welcome to anything they find in there.'

'They aren't fools, Fiona. They'll be knocking on Kay's door soon enough.'

'Aye. For all the good it'll do them. She won't say a word.'

'Is the other part in Scotland too?' I asked. 'Do you know?'

'It isn't in Hyde Park. I can tell you that much.'

The amusement died on her face as the door opened and Ivy came in. All of a sudden, she seemed uncomfortable, her expression guarded. Ivy registered the change and looked perplexed.

'It's all right,' I said to Fiona. 'You know she knows as much as I do.'

'And I won't say a word. I think it's great, what you did.'

Ivy was smiling but Fiona didn't relax. The tension persisted and there was an expression on her face that I couldn't read.

'Is there something else?' I asked.

When Fiona didn't answer, Ivy demanded, 'have I done something to offend you?'

'No. Not at all.'

'So what is it?' She had come in looking happier than she had for days but she was frowning now. 'What's wrong?'

Fiona looked at each of us in turn, dismayed, as if she was debating with herself whether to speak or not. Finally, she made up her mind.

'There's something you should know. Especially you, Ivy. And I'm sorry.'

Unease settled cold behind my ribs and I saw the flash of fear in Ivy's eyes.

'Go on.'

'I saw something. On the night of the murder. I couldn't sleep after Kay had gone. I was in my bedroom, watching the snow, and I saw someone come out of the trees on the other side of the drive, close to where Mr Coyle was found. He headed back to the house and for a minute, he looked towards the lodge.' She looked at her mother, as if she couldn't bear to speak the words to Ivy's face. 'It was Ben Newman.'

Jean drew in her breath. 'You never said—'

'I thought it was a bit odd at the time but nothing more. Then when the body was discovered...'

'You're sure it was Ben?' Ivy's voice was tight.

'He was caught in the light from my window and I saw him quite clearly.'

'What time was it?'

'Between three and four.'

Ivy backed away from us, as if trying to distance herself from what she had heard. She was deathly pale.

'I didn't want to tell you...'

'Ivy...' I moved towards her but she flung out a hand to stop me, turned on her heel and ran from the room.

'Poor wee lassie,' Jean began.

I didn't stay to hear more. I chased after Ivy, sick at heart and afraid for what would come next. She was halfway up the stairs and didn't stop when I called to her. By the time I reached her, she was on the landing outside her room.

'Wait. Ivy!'

She turned wild eyes in my direction, her face stricken.

'I believed him! What a fool I am!'

'No.'

'I went to him, Holly. I went to his room.'

I understood what she was telling me and my heart went out to her.

'There might be an explanation...'

'Stop it! Don't!'

We stood there, staring at each other in shock and misery.

'Oh, my darling.'

Her mouth twisted in pain. I turned to see Ben rounding the corner. When he saw us, he stopped dead in his tracks, his smile wiped off as if by a cloth.

'What is it?'

The look she gave him was as cold and hard as flint. 'Liar.'

'What's happened?'

'You swore to me you didn't do it.'

'That wasn't a lie.'

'You were seen. When you left Max's body by the wall. Fiona saw you.'

I saw the shock register in his eyes but he stood firm.

'It's not what it seems.'

'I don't believe you. How can I believe you?'

They both looked absolutely wretched and I was at the very end of my patience.

'Right,' I said firmly. 'In my room. Both of you. We're going to get to the bottom of this once and for all, whatever the consequences.'

When neither of them moved, I took Ivy's arm.

'I don't want to.'

There was fear in her voice and my heart smote me, but I steeled myself.

'This can't go on, darling. In you go.' I turned to Ben. 'And you.'

I opened the door and waved them in. None of us sat down. The atmosphere in the room was static with tension. Ivy was ashen, her eyes fierce. Ben raked a hand through his hair. I could see him trying to steady his breathing before he spoke.

'I didn't kill him.'

'No,' I said. 'That won't do. Enough denials. Explain to us simply, what were you doing when you were seen in the grounds at three o'clock in the morning? Tell us now or lose Ivy for good. That's your choice.'

One look at Ivy and he knew I was right. I watched as the fight went out of him.

'I moved the body.'

'You put him there? In that ditch?' Ivy's voice was barely audible.

'Yes. But I didn't kill him.'

'We need more from you,' I said. 'The whole story.'

He nodded his acquiescence.

'After I'd argued with Max outside Dorothy's door, I went to bed but I couldn't sleep. I went downstairs to get a book and a glass of scotch. I thought maybe I'd get a breath of air on the patio. There was a lamp lit in the dining room. Just enough light to see...' He stopped. His face was wracked with indecision, but I was merciless.

'Go on.'

'There was a dark heap on the ground. I went out and there he was, bleeding into the snow. There was someone standing by the body.'

'Who was it?'

'I promised not to say.'

'Oh for heaven's sake, we're way past all that! Spit it out.'

'Who was it, Ben?' Ivy repeated and it did the trick.

'It was Sonya.'

The name was wrenched from him, but we had it at last. To my shame, I felt a little rush of triumph. My number one suspect. It was the wife all along.

'Sonya murdered Max?'

'She asked me to help her,' he said simply. 'So I did.'

'Ben!' I stared at him, incredulous. 'What were you thinking?'

'I didn't want her to hang for killing a bastard like Coyle.'

I couldn't decide if he was a hero or a fool. I suppose it's possible to be both.

'She said if his body was dumped in the loch, it would probably never be found. He would just be reported missing. But he was too heavy for her to carry. I had to do that.'

'Dear God.' I sank into a chair.

'I was in my pyjamas so I grabbed some waterproofs from the boot room, shouldered him and headed for the gates.'

'But they were locked,' said Ivy heavily.

'I couldn't get out. The best I could do was hide the body in the grounds in the hope I could move it before lock-up the next night. But I didn't get the chance.'

'You idiot, Ben.' I was furious with him for getting into such a mess and with Sonya for dragging him into it. 'And what was Sonya doing whilst you were saving her bacon?'

'Cleaning up the patio. She washed it down with the outside hose. The snow covered it again before morning.'

'That's why it was so icy. Remember, Ivy? I slipped on it the next day.'

'I hosed down the coat and boots but the gloves were too far gone. I chucked them on my bedroom fire.'

'You knew he was there the whole time,' breathed Ivy. 'When we were searching...'

'I hated hiding it from you.' Ben took a step towards Ivy, but she recoiled in horror. It was clear how much it hurt him. I thought for a minute he was going to break down completely but he held himself together and carried on. 'Sonya begged me to give her some time to get away. We had no idea we'd be snowed in by daylight. Just stuck here. Waiting.'

'So that was the plan, that she would make a run for it as soon as she could? And what about you? You've made yourself an accessory. Were you going to disappear too?'

'No. I planned to stick it out and say nothing.'

I threw my hands in the air.

'For a clever man, you have been extraordinarily stupid.'

'I know.' He sagged like a punctured tyre and dropped onto the arm of my chair. 'And then this morning, I thought the bullets were for me, to keep me quiet for good. I thought the less you knew, the safer you'd be.'

'Sonya shot at us?' Ivy's eyes flashed in her pale face. 'Is she completely mad?'

'She says it was all for show. To warn you off. To take me off your suspect list. That's her story anyway. She says she's a crack shot and we were never in danger. I told her she was a dangerous hothead.'

'When did she say that?' I asked.

'Just now.'

'Where?'

'In her room.'

'You left her there?' I jumped to my feet. I was ready for some serious words with Sonya Stirling.

'Yes.'

'Well, she isn't there now.' Ivy was looking out of the window. We both joined her, just in time to see Sonya's Super Eight speed down the drive and out of the gates. 'What does she think she's doing? The roads are still blocked. She won't get anywhere.'

'She's driving too fast,' breathed Ben. 'She'll come a cropper.'

'Come on.' I ran to the door. 'I'm sorry, Ben, it's all got to come out now. We need to find Andrew.'

He put up no resistance. The two of them followed me down into the hall. Things had come to a head and I didn't know how to feel about it. A little unworthy part of me was disappointed that the chase was over, but mostly I was anxious, for Sonya's safety, for Ben's future and for Ivy's happiness. However things unfolded from here, it wouldn't be good. It seemed we were wedded to calamity.

'Was that Sonya?' Andrew was standing at the open door, with Esme. 'What on earth is she playing at?'

'Can't you guess?' I asked and saw realisation dawn in both their faces.

'Oh God.' Esme threw out a hand and I took it.

'Somebody needs to go after her.'

Andrew was out on the steps before I finished speaking. He disappeared around the corner of the house, towards the garages.

'Your car is a mile away,' Esme called after him.

'I'll take yours.'

'Be careful! It's still icy.'

We watched as the car appeared on the drive and was quickly through the gates and out of sight. When it was gone, Esme closed the door but we didn't move from the hall. It was as if we were rooted to the spot. Turning back I saw Ivy and Ben on either side of the wide staircase. He was staring across at her. She was avoiding his eyes. They looked battered and my heart bled for them.

'What's going on?' Elliot appeared at the gallery rail, taking me back to our arrival on Christmas Eve, when we stood in this beautiful house for the first time, looking forward to the days ahead, blissfully ignorant of what was to come.

'We should gather in the drawing room.' Esme came to life. 'Elliot, can you find Dorothy? Holly, darling, would you fetch Godfrey from his room? I'll get the MacRaes.'

I did as she asked and ten minutes later we were all together in an uneasy group, everyone waiting to hear a car engine, watching the drive for the return of Andrew and Sonya. After the first reactions of incredulity, there was little or no conversation. Shock silenced us and we were all alone with our thoughts.

Ben and Ivy were at opposite ends of the room, as far apart as it was possible to be. Godfrey and Elliot sat either side of the fire, Esme was on a sofa with Ishbel and Dorothy and the MacRaes were standing in the dining room doorway, a little apart, as they had been the whole time – not quite guests, not quite staff. A tight little unit all their own. What must they think of us? Silly and shallow purveyors of make believe. Spoilt. Cosseted. And in at least one case, dangerous. I gave myself a shake to dispel my dark thoughts.

At last, after what seemed like an age, a car made its way up the driveway. It was Andrew's and still in one piece, thank the lord. Sonya was in the passenger seat. Perhaps her beautiful Packard hadn't escaped so luckily. They didn't go around to the garages but parked by the porch. As Sonya climbed out, she glanced towards the drawing room windows and the tension around me became unbearable. Esme clutched at Ishbel, Fiona took her mother's arm, Ivy got to her feet and Ben's pale face lost its last vestige of colour. With my heart thundering in my chest, I heard the main door open and close and footsteps cross the hall. Every head turned as they came into the room.

37

IVY

I could feel his gaze fastened on me but I couldn't look at him. The image of him carrying Max Coyle's bleeding body through the snow was burning behind my eyes. I knew he had done the wrong thing for the right reasons, that his intentions were good. I knew now that he wasn't a murderer and that was no small relief. But it had cast a shadow that I was struggling to brush away. He was complicated. Sam was so easy to love compared to Ben.

Not that I didn't feel for him as we all waited in the drawing room. If I felt like I was walking on hot coals, how much worse must it be for him?

When Sonya finally appeared, I couldn't sit still. I stood up and then felt conspicuous and wished I'd stayed in my chair. In fact, I doubt anyone noticed. Everyone was intent on Sonya Stirling, who crossed to the fireplace and helped herself to a cigarette with more composure than the rest of us put together. She leant against the mantlepiece and surveyed her audience with a practised eye.

'I'm sorry for the drama,' she drawled. 'My car is in a ditch but I'm unscathed. I'd hoped to save you all this little scene but the roads are still too icy for speed.' She gave us her legendary smile. 'So here we are.'

She was formidable, whatever her sins. I've no idea what I would have done in her position but I wouldn't have carried it off like she did, that's for sure. Few people could. The silence that followed was proof of how thoroughly she had taken the wind out of everyone's sails. It must have been a good minute before Holly sprang to life and broke the spell. Of course she was the one to do it.

'For pity's sake, Sonya!' she exclaimed. 'I don't know whether to slap you or give you a cheer.'

Sonya raised an elegant eyebrow. 'Let me know when you decide.'

She exhaled and the smoke curled around her face and head. She looked like the heroine in a scene from a Philip Marlowe film, and the realisation washed over me that she was playing a part. Of course she was. Sonya Stirling was acting her socks off. I wondered if every second in her company was a performance, if she was ever her true self. If she knew who her true self was anymore.

Esme rose from the sofa to stand at Andrew's side by the window. There were two spots of colour in her pale cheeks and a cold fury in her eyes that took me by surprise. Holly always said that Esme was tough as hickory but this was my first real glimpse of it. She saw a threat to her home and family and every nerve in her body was on alert to defend them. She turned on Sonya, like a tiger defending her young.

'Amusing as this repartee is, I've got a lot of questions that need answers, if that's all right with you?'

I felt the tension in the room go up a notch. With all eyes on her, Sonya had the good grace to acknowledge the reprimand with a slight nod of the head.

'How much do you know?' she asked.

'Just that you made a run for it and Andrew had to risk life and limb going after you.'

'I didn't have much of a choice.' She looked across at Ben. 'Lover boy here was going to spill the beans at last.'

'Ben? What has he got to do with it?'

Holly sought out my eyes across the room, asking permission to speak and getting it.

'She dragged him into her mess,' she said. 'You used him, Sonya. It was unforgivable.'

'She didn't force me.' Ben's voice was quiet but level. 'I agreed to it.'

'She took advantage of your good nature.'

'This is getting us nowhere.' Andrew spoke at last. 'We need the full story. Ben first, then Sonya. Everyone else, try not to interrupt. Let's get to the bottom of this once and for all. We're owed that, at least.'

Everyone was glad for Andrew to take charge, as the owner of Black Gairy and our host. Attention turned on Ben. I saw him take a breath in, steadying himself. A lock of hair fell over his eyes and I wanted to brush it back. Every part of me ached to touch him.

'I found Sonya with the body. On the terrace. She asked me to help her move it.'

He told his story again, quietly and calmly, without making excuses for himself. He faced their shock and condemnation and he never once looked at me, not for a second. I don't know what I would have done if he had.

When he was finished, Esme turned to Sonya. 'What would have happened if Ben hadn't arrived?'

'I'd have left Max where he was, I guess. No way could I carry him. I don't know. Ben came along and I saw a way out.'

'You shot at us!' Holly exclaimed.

'I was trying to help. I could see that Ivy here suspected Ben was a murderer. I thought it would establish his innocence.' Sonya laughed. 'Crazy plan.'

'You're mad. You could have killed us.'

'No way. You were never in danger. I grew up on a ranch in Montana. I could take an apple off your head at 200 yards.' She turned to Esme and Andrew. 'Look, I'm sorry for all of it. I thought we could lose the body in the loch and all go our separate ways leaving the disappearance of Max Coyle as an unsolved mystery. It didn't work out that way.'

'Shame.' It was Elliot's voice. 'It was a good plan.'

'Not funny,' said Esme.

'Not meant to be.'

'Enough now.' Andrew took his wife's hand. 'Some respect is due.'

'He never showed any,' said Dorothy.

Andrew didn't rise to it.

'Tomorrow Donald and I will walk to the police station in Newton Stewart.' He turned to Sonya. 'I'm sorry but we have to deal with this.'

'I'm sorry you didn't get away.' Dorothy was defiant.

'It was worth a try.' Sonya smiled.

'Will Ben be charged too?' asked Ishbel from the sofa.

There was an awkward silence, broken by Fiona.

'Aye,' she said. 'Accessory after the fact.'

Ben looked at me then. I searched for fear in his eyes but

didn't find any. What I saw was strength. And love for me. Without another thought, I crossed the room, stood by his side and took his hand. I could be strong too and I needed him to know that. He didn't say anything but he intertwined his fingers with mine and held on tight. And that was that. We both knew that whatever he had to face now, he wouldn't do it alone.

'What an awful mess,' said Esme. 'Oh Sonya, why did you have to do it?'

Sonya Stirling was stubbing out her cigarette, carefully and thoroughly.

'Well, that's the thing,' she said quietly and then she looked up with a strange smile on her face. 'Truth is, y'all, I didn't do it.'

We all stared at her in astonishment.

'What do you mean?' Esme asked blankly.

'Just what I said, honey. I didn't kill him. It wasn't me.'

38

HOLLY

'Do you believe her?' asked Ivy.

We were in my room. Outside the light was fading on another day and, after all the drama, we still hadn't found the killer. Sonya was sticking to her new story. She found Max dead on the terrace. No, she didn't see who did it. No, she wasn't prepared to explain why she took the blame. The more we spluttered and raged, the calmer she became. She was unmovable. Eventually, Andrew drew the interrogation to a close.

'Well, the police will be here tomorrow. Perhaps they'll be better at getting some sense out of you. Meantime, I suggest you confine yourself to your room. We'll have some food sent up.'

'Am I under arrest?'

'You should be,' said Ben grimly. 'I thought I was helping you.'

'You were. I wanted the body to disappear.'

'But why? If you didn't kill him?'

She just smiled slightly.

At Ben's side, Ivy was taut with anger.

'So you're in the clear but you've made Ben an accessory. It's unforgivable!'

'I'm sorry for that. Really.'

'Oh, you're impossible!' I exclaimed in frustration.

'And I washed down the patio, don't forget, so not totally in the clear.'

'We're going round in circles again,' said Esme. 'Just go upstairs, Sonya. Please. Just go away.'

For a fleeting second, Sonya looked shamefaced. It was gone in an instant, but I caught it in her eyes before the mask was back in place. She was very fond of Esme and sorry to cause her pain. I believed that much was true. After the briefest of pauses, she gave a little bow and walked out of the room without a look back. The door closed behind her and the rest of us stared at each other in silence. It really was too much to absorb. My head was reeling.

'What on earth is she playing at?' I asked no one in particular.

'Damn the woman.' Andrew drew Esme into him and kissed her hair.

Elliot voiced the question at the back of all our minds.

'The thing is,' he drawled, looking at all our tense faces, 'if she's telling the truth and she didn't kill him, then who did?'

It was the strangest sensation. No one moved but I felt everyone withdraw into themselves. I felt their defences go up.

'Not now, man,' snapped Andrew.

'Not helpful,' murmured Godfrey.

'I'm only saying what you're all thinking.'

'Please be quiet, Elliot.' Esme looked sick and tired of all of us and I can't say I blamed her. 'Let's just get through tonight, shall we? The police will ask enough questions tomorrow.'

Elliot shrugged.

'Very well. In which case, I shall withdraw to my quarters. I don't know about the rest of you but I feel the need to lie down in a darkened room.'

His departure was the signal for a breakup of the gathering. The MacRaes left together, Ishbel joined her father and Esme by the window, Dorothy linked arms with Godfrey and walked him across the hall, Ivy and Ben slipped into the library and I climbed the stairs to my room and dropped onto my bed like a dead weight, utterly spent. The day had been relentless. At some point I dozed off. When I opened my eyes again it was dusk and Ivy was lying on the chaise, staring out of the window.

'You look miles away,' I said to her.

She came out of her reverie with a start.

'Plenty to think about,' she said.

'You can say that again!'

'You were fast asleep. I didn't want to disturb you.'

'Thank you, darling. You can put on a light now.'

She reached over, switched on a table lamp and sat in its yellow glow, her legs curled under her, a bent arm supporting her chin. I thought of a snapshot I begged from her years ago, taken when she was eight, eating ice cream with her sisters on Morecambe Pier. The other two were smiling, but Ivy was caught in a moment of intense curiosity and determination, staring out at the world, taking it on. I love that photograph. I love it when I see the same expression on her grown-up face. It was there now in the lamplight.

'So where do we go from here?' she asked.

Leaning back against my propped-up pillows, I shook my head.

'You tell me, darling. I'm at my wit's end.'

'I could cheerfully throttle Sonya.'

'Join the queue!'

'Do you believe her?'

I threw my arms wide.

'Which story? Which version?'

'Did she kill Max? And if not, does she really not know who did?'

I took a minute to examine my thoughts, weigh my gut feeling.

'I have absolutely no idea,' I said.

'Thank you for your contribution.'

'My pleasure.'

Ivy unfolded her legs and sat forward.

'I was putting my thoughts in order whilst you were asleep. There's a lot we don't know but some things are clear now. He was killed on the patio, not long after three in the morning. Ben moved the body and Sonya cleaned up the evidence.' She looked up at me. 'I think we've got the truth from Ben now. I think we can cross him off the list. Do you?'

'Yes, darling.' I gave her a smile. 'That's good news.'

'He's an idiot but he isn't a murderer.'

'It was a gallant act.'

'It was reckless. And a bit disturbing.'

'He's a complex man.'

She was silent for a moment and I saw fear creep into her eyes.

'He's determined to tell the police everything. He might go to jail.'

'If the worst happens, then we'll face it and find a way through,' I said. 'We know how to do that.' I was trying to give some comfort but realised how pessimistic I sounded and searched instead for some hopeful words. It wasn't easy in the circumstances. 'But we don't know what will unfold, do we?'

'That much is true. It's impenetrable. My brain is whirling like a windmill. It's driving me mad.' She stood up and shook herself like a wet dog. When she looked across at me, it was with a vestige of her old spirit.

'Better?' I asked.

'Not a lot.'

I got up from the bed and surveyed myself in the mirror. I had dozed in my clothes and was a crumpled mess.

'What's happening about dinner, I wonder?'

'What Jean MacRae calls a cold collation,' said Ivy. 'Help yourself and feel free to eat in your room. No one wants to gather round a table tonight.'

'I'll second that. What a shambles.'

'Well, the police will take over tomorrow.'

'But will they? If the roads are still blocked? Andrew and Donald will be walking over 20 miles there and back. I don't envy them.'

'Snow ploughs maybe? At any rate, it will be out of our hands.'

I turned from the mirror and raised an eyebrow.

'Are you as relieved as you sound?'

She thought for a minute before she answered.

'I don't know. Part of me wants to solve it and the other half wants to abdicate responsibility.'

I understood. But still I couldn't let it go.

'I'll tell you one thing. I don't believe for a minute that Sonya just stumbled on the body.'

'Me neither,' Ivy agreed. 'Either she did it or she knows who did and is protecting them. But why would she? Apart from Esme, she barely knows anyone here.'

'Who would she feel protective of? Or indebted to? Neither option sounds very much like Sonya to me.'

'Well, like it or not, she's got the answer and she's keeping it to herself.'

I installed myself in my chair, looking out at the view. Night had fallen and the grounds were silver in the moonlight, criss-crossed with dark shadows. Despite the beauty on show, I found myself longing for the sights and sounds of my own home: London rooftops and the glow of streetlights, the hum of traffic in the streets, the anonymity of strangers. I had to force my mind back to the task at hand.

'Shall we look at the list?' I asked. 'It's been a while.'

We settled ourselves down to work our way through the names again. It felt like a long journey since we had first written them down and we had uncovered so many secrets, buried and hidden, like the ground under the snow outside. In the same way that snowfall changes the landscape, renders it strangely unfamiliar, these people I thought I knew would never look quite the same to me again.

'Right,' said Ivy. 'What do we know? Max was alive on the top landing at three. Less than an hour later, he was dead on the patio. Who could have done it? First name – Andrew.'

'Esme says he was in bed with her but he might have slipped out whilst she was sleeping. Or she could be lying.'

'Do you think she would?' Ivy looked up at me, surprised and solemn. 'That wrecks their joint alibi.'

'My heart says no,' I told her, 'but our doubts are traitors. Let's keep both of them in play for now.'

'And Ishbel?'

'We know she has a secret to keep. What if Max found out?'

'Well, that's true for Elliot too. And all the MacRaes.'

'This is getting us nowhere!' I raked a hand through my hair. 'Who *wasn't* he a threat to?'

'That we know of, you mean? Well, there's Ben – please God, we've got the full story from him now. And Godfrey. We haven't uncovered anything between him and Max, apart from general loathing, have we?'

'He says he left Max and Andrew on the patio at about two. Have we any reason not to believe him?'

'I don't think so. It's really affected him though. He seems frailer.'

Ivy frowned with frustration. 'Why would Sonya take the blame for any of them? It doesn't make sense.'

'She owed Dorothy a good turn,' I mused. 'For the Max business. But surely that's disproportionate?'

'Dorothy?' I could see Ivy's thoughts racing. She was folding and refolding the piece of paper in her hand. 'You might say she had the most obvious motive. The most immediate.'

'She asked about the *sgian dubh*.'

'Yes. She did.'

'And she's a different girl since his death.'

'Aye.'

'But you aren't convinced?'

223

Ivy looked up from her origami. She had made a paper plane and with a swift motion of her arm, she let it fly, watching it glide and fall to the floor.

'I don't know.' She sighed. 'I can't get rid of the nagging worry that even with everything we've discovered, we haven't found the real motive yet. Something that would explain Sonya's behaviour, fit the pieces together.'

'Or she stabbed him and she's playing games.'

'Which brings us full circle.'

We looked at each other in silence for a long moment.

'Are we beaten?' I asked at last.

Ivy didn't reply. She walked over and picked up the grounded plane from the rug. Unfolding it, she stared down at the contents with fierce concentration.

'We're missing something.'

I had my answer. She wasn't giving up. We were as stubborn as each other.

'Once more unto the breach, then,' I said.

39

Elliot Mayhew was lying on his bed, half-asleep, when he was roused by a tap on the door. Surprised and curious, he got to his feet. No one came to his room, except Jean MacRae or Esme to bring clean towels, but a fresh supply had arrived earlier in the day, so that wasn't the case. He smoothed down his hair and clothes and opened up, to find Dorothy Drake in the doorway with an envelope in her hand.

'I think this is yours.' She held it out with an awkward smile. 'I'm not proud of how it came into my hands, but I'm glad to be able to return it to you.'

He knew what it was instantly and the tide of relief that washed over him left him dizzy. Leaning against the door frame, he stared at her in amazement.

'How...?'

'Please don't ask me how I got it. Just take it. With my best wishes.'

He took it from her in a daze, opened it and stared at the few sentences on the page; foolish words of passion that had haunted his life for years. Back in his hands. He was safe at last.

'I don't know what to say. Which is very rare.'

'I had to read it,' she said solemnly. 'Just quickly, to know who it belonged to. But I'll never breathe a word of it. I promise.'

'I'm in your debt.'

'No.' She shook her head. 'Just forget it.'

'I never will.'

She took a quick breath.

'I stole it. From his briefcase. He left it open to take a phone call and I grabbed a fistful of his papers and ran. Hoping there would be something to use against him, to loosen his grip.'

'And then someone loosened it for good.'

'Yes.'

'I stole the whole bloody briefcase. Smashed it open. But you got there first.'

Their eyes met and they laughed.

'Two wrongs made a right this time,' said Dorothy.

'Thank you.'

She nodded and walked away. Elliot closed the door, crossed to the fire and threw the letter into the flames. He watched it flare and disappear and then he sat on the edge of his bed and stared out at the starry sky. The tears, when they came, hot and silent, were equal parts regret and relief.

40

Ishbel was hovering on the galleried landing, looking down into the hall below. She knew her father was in his study and she knew she had to go down and join him but, once again, her courage failed her. She loved him. She couldn't bear to lose him. She shrank from the thought that a few words from her could estrange them forever.

As she watched, the study door opened. Donald and Jean MacRae came out, pausing in the doorway to look back at Andrew, who she could just see in the room behind them. All three had solemn faces. Donald put his arm around Jean and they moved across the hall with Andrew watching them thoughtfully before he closed the door again.

As he did, Godfrey came out of his room next to the library. Unaware of Ishbel's scrutiny, he approached the study and hesitated at the door, leaning on his silver-topped cane, indecision in his face. Apparently her father was in demand that afternoon. But after a few seconds, the old man moved on towards the drawing room and disappeared from sight.

Ishbel took a deep breath and released her white-knuckled grip on the gallery rail. Tomorrow the police would start asking questions. All the lives at Black Gairy would be investigated and secrets would come to light. Better to tell it now, in the way she wanted it told. Better to have some control. At long last, with her heart in her mouth, she went down to see her father.

41

IVY

Me and Ben were curled up on my bed, my head on his shoulder, his hand in my hair. A few minutes together, away from murder and all its repercussions. It was still there, waiting for us outside my bedroom door, but we were keeping it at bay for a few precious minutes, being normal, just being us.

'Did you like being a librarian?' he asked.

'I liked being around books. But I like being a dresser better.'

'Never a dull moment, I imagine.'

'With Holly? You can say that again.' I snuggled up to him, breathing him in. 'How did you come to be writing plays?'

'In the Young Communists. I got dragged into the Workers Theatre and I can't act for toffee so I ended up writing sketches and stuff and it grew from there.'

'Sam was in the Labour Youth for a while.'

'But not you?'

'I was never a joiner.'

He laughed and kissed the end of my nose.

'Don't ever change, Ivy.'

'It's not likely.'

'Good.'

'Doesn't mean I don't want a better world, though.'

'I know. Me too.'

We lapsed into a happy silence. It was ridiculous, given the circumstances, but I couldn't stop smiling. For ten years I'd built a wall, brick by brick. Bricks of love and grief and loyalty and fear. It kept me safe. I was fine. And then I took a sledgehammer to it. I stood among the rubble and reached out for Ben. I wasn't safe anymore. I was back in the world of risk and danger, I was wide open, and I should have been scared to death, but I wasn't. Whatever came next, I was ready for it. Never more sure of anything. What a turn up, Ivy. Never say never.

I looked up at him.

'Read to me.'

'What from?'

'Holly's Christmas present.' I nodded towards the Burns on the bedside table. 'How's your Scottish accent?'

'Terrible.'

'I'll make allowances.'

'You'll need to.'

I raised my head and kissed his cheek. 'Go on, then.'

Of course he chose 'A man's a man for a' that.'

> *'For a' that, an' a' that,*
> *Their tinsel show, an' a' that;*
> *The honest man, tho' e'er sae poor,*
> *Is king o' men for a' that.'*

Outside the window, the sky was dark above a still and silent blanket of snow. The solid pink walls of Black Gairy held us cocooned, safe from the weather, safe from the world. Burns' words rang through the centuries and my hand on Ben's heart rose and fell with his breathing.

He finished reading and closed the book.

'It's a beautiful edition,' he said, admiring the old leather binding. 'My copy isn't so fine.'

'You've got one?'

'A present from an old comrade in Stepney. Archie MacDougal. He's Glasgow born and bred and worships Rabbie.'

'Should I know the name?' I asked. 'It sounds familiar.'

'Did you read up on the Fedorov Conspiracy after Sonya's melodramatics? He was one of the five arrested on trumped-up charges.'

'No, I didn't.'

'Oh, I know what it will be. He stood for Parliament in '35. Contested Mile End for the Communists. He didn't win but there was a lot of publicity at the time, because of his history. None of it good, naturally.'

'That must be it. So he knew the girl who died? What exactly happened to her?'

'They were accused of conspiring with the Russians to infiltrate the Labour Party. A fake letter was published from a non-existent Russian spy and hysteria was whipped up. It was only a few years after the Russian Revolution and there were Red Scares everywhere. A mob descended on the office of the Young Communist League and somebody lobbed a brick through the window which hit Harry and broke her skull.'

'How terrible. And your friend Archie was there?'

'He was involved with Harry. They were together.'

'Oh, Ben.'

'He never got over her, really. He talked about her for years. His Ettie. That was his name for her.'

'Ettie?'

'From Henrietta.'

'Oh. I assumed Harry was short for Harriet…'

I stopped talking and sat bolt upright.

'What?' asked Ben. 'What is it?'

'Henrietta?'

'Yes.'

'Bloody hell!'

I remembered hearing the name from Holly. A long dead girl. A grieving father. Was that the answer at last? Certain I was right, I scrambled off the bed, leaving Ben staring in surprise.

'Ivy?'

'Sorry,' I called back, as I ran through the bathroom to its other door. 'I need to talk to Holly.'

42

HOLLY

'Oh God!' I stared at Ivy in utter dismay.

She had tumbled into my room from the bathroom, her face alight with excitement at the news she had to share. But she quickly sobered as we both realised we finally had the truth and it was awful.

Everything slotted into place. The Stone of Destiny, the sexual advances, the infidelity, the blackmail, all the secrets we had uncovered were just distractions. The past, in the shape of young Harry Parker, had caught up with Max Coyle at Black Gairy. We had our murderer and there was nothing to feel but grief.

'What do we do now?' she asked.

'We go together to see him. To hear it in his words.' I shook my head, at a total loss. 'After that, I have no idea.'

As we walked down the stairs, Ivy reached for my hand and we stayed clasped together till we reached his door. I used my free hand to knock and he called from inside.

'Come in.'

She loosened her grasp then and I felt like I was adrift on a wide sea. I took a deep breath and opened the door.

Godfrey was sitting in the winged armchair. In the light from the bedside lamp, he looked gaunt and weary. I'd known him for so many years and never thought of him as an old man, but I saw his age now, in the deep lines of his face and the hollows of his eyes as he turned to greet us. I watched as he read our expressions and as his own altered. He knew we knew, but he didn't look afraid. He held out a hand and I took it, sitting on the bed by his side.

'There was no riding accident, was there?'

He shook his head.

'She was murdered. An ignorant thug threw the brick but Max Coyle put it in his hand. Harry Parker was my beloved girl. She had her stepfather's name. I didn't know she existed until she was sixteen and she came to find me. I only had three years with her.' He gave me a smile that broke my heart. 'She was extraordinary. So full of hope and passion. She had so much to give. And it was all ripped away.'

'I'm so sorry.'

'I had no idea, until Sonya's speech on Christmas Day, that Coyle was behind the scurrilous lies that killed her. I was in utter shock. I don't know how I got through the evening. I drank a great deal.'

I remembered that Christmas dinner. Laughing with Esme and teasing Godfrey and, all the time, he was nursing that agony in his heart. Ivy and I stared at each other in horror.

'When everyone had gone to bed, I confronted him on the terrace. He denied responsibility. 'How did I know it would happen?' was all he said. No remorse. No humanity. I reached down for his *sgian dubh* and plunged it into his neck.'

Godfrey was in tears but he told his story calmly and quietly. He seemed relieved. What a burden he had been carrying for the last few days.

'It was over in minutes,' he said. 'Anyone who fought in the trenches knows how to cut a throat. I left him where he fell and went to my room, expecting to confess the next morning when the body was discovered. But when I came back at dawn, the terrace was clear. No body. No blood. Just a fresh fall of pure white snow. I was mystified. For a few moments, I wondered if I'd dreamt the whole thing, but I knew I hadn't. I knew I had killed him.'

He was silent at last. His hand was still in mine, the hand that had brushed the hair from his dying child's face, the hand that had plunged a dagger into Max Coyle's neck. For a long moment, none of us moved. It seemed that time was frozen. I felt numb. Heavy with the pity of it all.

When I finally spoke, it came out as a whisper.

'What now? What happens now?'

Godfrey stirred into life.

'Ivy, will you gather everyone in the drawing room?'

I heard her quick intake of breath.

'You're going to tell them?'

'It's time.'

'But...' I began.

'It's time, my dear. Please, Ivy. If you will.'

She nodded and left the room. Godfrey reached for his cane and got to his feet. I wanted to turn back time, never to have known what I knew. I wanted to take it all away. Why did we play detective? Why on earth did we meddle?

'I'm so sorry,' I told him. 'For all of it.'

'I know,' said Godfrey. 'So am I.'

*

Ivy had assembled everyone in the drawing room. All eyes turned towards Godfrey and I as we came through from the hall. He had his walking cane but he stood upright as he surveyed the room, his white hair swept back from his brow, his furrowed old face defiant. I thought he looked magnificent. Like King Lear.

Ivy was standing with Ben by the fireplace, pale and solemn. The rest of the party were scattered in twos and threes, expectant and apprehensive. Godfrey didn't keep them waiting. He repeated his story simply and steadily. Then, in the stunned silence that followed, he turned to Esme and Andrew.

'I can never make amends for the grief I've caused in your beautiful home. I apologise to you – and to you all – from the bottom of my heart, for putting you through this ordeal.' His face hardened. 'But I am not sorry I put an end to that monstrous man. I will never be sorry for that.'

With his task completed, he seemed to lose all strength and sagged over his cane, flinging out an arm to me for support. I helped him to a chair and he sank into it and leant back heavily.

I looked from face to face as the silence continued. Above everything else, there was a strange anticlimax now that the truth was out. I think we were all shell-shocked, slow to react.

The first to come to life was Ben. With dawning anger in his face, he confronted Sonya.

'So why did you tell me you did it?'

She faced him, unrepentant. 'I couldn't sleep so I came down to find Max, to yell at him, let off some steam. He was outside on the terrace with Godfrey and I could hear from what they were saying that I'd revealed a devastating secret.' She turned to Godfrey. 'I was trying to hurt Max and I hurt you instead. I saw you stab him and I knew it was my fault.'

'So you took the blame.'

'It was an impulse. You left without seeing me in the shadows. I went out and he was lying there dead. Ben appeared and I thought, maybe I could pull it off, maybe I could give you a way out. I owed you.'

'No, my dear. None of that. The responsibility is all mine.'

'I don't regret it. I'd do it again.'

'Thanks,' said Ben drily.

'I didn't mean for you to get hit so hard. I was happy to disappear, leaving everyone to believe I did it. But the snow. The goddamned snow trapped me here.'

'Oh, Sonya,' I sighed.

It was a grand gesture. Generous and brave, irresponsible and gloriously egocentric. Sonya Stirling in a nutshell.

'So case closed.' Elliot spoke from the sofa where he was sitting with Dorothy. 'And what happens now?'

'I'm ready to face the consequences,' said Godfrey quietly. 'Andrew and Donald can give the police my confession tomorrow. I'll go quietly, as they say.'

'Oh, Godfrey.' Esme left Andrew's side and came towards us. She crouched before his chair and grasped both of his hands.

'I haven't lost your friendship?' he asked her.

Choked with tears, she shook her head and echoed my earlier words.

'I wish I could make it all go away.'

'I don't ask for that.'

'I'm sorry, Godfrey.' Andrew spoke for the first time. 'It's a rotten business but...'

'But a man is dead. A life was taken and a price must be paid.'

Andrew nodded. Esme got to her feet and planted a kiss on Godfrey's brow. Over his head, we shared a look of helpless sorrow. Justice would run its course now but the thought of it broke my heart. I knew that no one deserved to die as Max did. I knew Godfrey was a murderer. I knew it but I couldn't bear it. I looked across at Ivy in desperation and she took a step towards me, but Dorothy's voice brought her to a standstill.

'Why?' She was sitting forward in her chair, her young face earnest. 'Why must a price be paid? Who says so?'

'Now then, lassie.' Jean MacRae, standing beside her, laid a motherly hand on her shoulder.

'No one is happy with this,' Andrew said, 'but there's a dead body in my summer house and we have to do the right thing.'

'But what is the right thing? That's what I'm asking.' She turned to Ben. 'You moved the body. You would have dropped it in the lake if you could. Was that right or wrong?'

'Honestly? I don't know.' He paused, as if searching for a better answer. 'It felt like I was doing the wrong thing for the right reason.'

'Ivy?' Dorothy shifted her gaze. 'What do you think?'

I watched Ivy intently, wondering if she felt as Dorothy did, as I did. Sudden hope clutched at my heart, followed quickly by fear. We were treading dangerous ground now. Ivy brushed a dark curl from her forehead and met Dorothy's eyes.

'I'm asking myself,' she said steadily, 'what purpose it would serve to send Godfrey to prison?'

'The law—' Andrew began but Elliot interrupted him.

'The law is an ass,' he drawled. 'And Max Coyle was a monster. Sorry, Sonya.'

'Not necessary. You're right.'

'Well,' said Ishbel, 'I don't want to see Godfrey arrested.' She was standing with her father and when he looked at her in astonishment, she smiled and touched his arm. 'Come on, Dad. This isn't the biggest shock I've given you today, is it?'

I saw the look that passed between them then and one glance at Esme confirmed my suspicion that they had been told about Jack. Good for Ishbel. She had taken the first step on a long road and I was happy for her. Poor Andrew, however, was having his assumptions challenged for the second time in one day and he looked shell-shocked. I felt sorry for him.

'Esme?' He turned to his wife.

Her eyes were fixed on Godfrey, her Madonna's face pale and solemn.

'Is there a way?' She seemed to be asking the room. 'What can we do?'

'Well, my original plan wasn't a bad one,' Sonya answered. 'Lose him in the loch.'

'Dear lord!' Andrew raised his eyes to the ceiling. 'Are you actually considering...'

'Somewhere he'll never be found,' said Dorothy. 'No body, no case. What's it called, Fiona?'

'Habeas Corpus.'

'And the legal term for what we would be doing?' asked Andrew heavily.

'Perverting the course of justice.'

'And the penalty for that?'

'It could be a custodial sentence.'

'Marvellous. So we all go to jail!'

Dorothy didn't flinch. 'Not if we have a plan and stick to it. And stick together.' She was calm and confident. What a way she has travelled since Christmas Eve. 'But we all have to agree, of course. All of us.'

'Count me in,' said Sonya shortly.

'And me,' added Elliot.

Dorothy looked at the rest of us, waiting for an answer.

'I think we should,' I found myself saying.

Ben and Ivy nodded their assent and then Ishbel. Esme gave her husband an apologetic smile.

'Yes,' she said. 'If Andrew agrees.'

'It's madness.'

'I know.'

He turned to the MacRaes.

'It isn't fair to drag you three into this. What do you think? Tell us honestly.'

I watched them curiously. They had reasons of their own for wanting to stay clear of the police just now. A missing person is less sensational than a murder, of course, but would it mean less scrutiny or more?

'Donald can take the boat out tonight,' Jean said simply.

'I ken a spot or two in the loch where nothing will ever be found. There's nae worry about that.'

'But we need to get our story straight.' Fiona was practical, as ever. 'The best lies are based round the truth. We tell the police exactly what happened up until we found the body. He wasn't missed for most of Boxing Day. We assumed he was still in bed, or off looking for a working phone. Sonya thought he slept elsewhere. Dad and Andrew walked to the village and then we all went out looking for him. So far, so good.'

'Then we just skip the bit where we found him,' said Sonya. 'We've no idea where he is. For all we know he walked to Newton Stewart and got a train home. It's the sort of thing he would have done, the bastard.'

'Steady on.'

'Don't speak ill of the dead? Why not?'

'We're talking about sinking him into the loch without ceremony.' Andrew spoke sharply. 'The least we can do is show a little respect.'

'Is that you agreeing?' asked Elliot.

Andrew frowned and Esme crossed to him and took his arm.

'If you feel you can't do it, you must say so. You have every right to say no. You most of all, here in our home. Whatever you decide, darling, I'm with you.'

He hesitated, looking deeply into her face, his love for her written clearly on his own.

'I know how fond you are of Godfrey...' he began.

'My dears, this must stop now.' Godfrey's rich voice was

resolved. 'I am so grateful that you would even consider risking yourselves for me, but it won't do.'

There was a general protest, all eyes on the old man looking back at us with a calm dignity that squeezed my heart. We entreated but he raised both palms and shook his head.

'Thank you. All of you. But I can't allow it.'

'Godfrey.' I took his hand.

'It's no use, Elspeth. Bless you, but no.'

He was determined and it seemed settled. I don't think I was alone in being close to tears of sadness and frustration. But life is full of surprises. It was Andrew who turned the tide. Andrew, the reluctant conspirator, turned from Esme's wretched eyes with a slight smile that stopped us all in our tracks.

'Look at the faces of your friends, Godfrey. We are all affected by these events. We are all deeply unsettled and in need of some peace, some kind of justice.' He took a breath. 'I was slower to realise what everyone else felt instinctively. Some good must come from this. Something must be salvaged. You have to let us help you, as much for our sakes as for yours.'

There was a breathless moment as Godfrey looked from face to face.

'You all feel this way?'

There was a general assent.

'If he is never found, the investigation will drag on, become a *cause célèbre*.'

'Scandal has a short memory, honey,' said Sonya. 'Take it from one who knows.'

'If suspicion ever fell on any of you, I would make a full

confession. How I killed him and how I disposed of the body single-handedly.'

'You expect them to believe you got him into the loch all by yourself?'

'You will all feign ignorance and that is the only story they will get. I'll also put it in writing, to be opened after my death, if necessary.'

'Does this mean...?'

Under his white brows, Godfrey's eyes filled with tears.

'If we agree to my terms, then with love and gratitude, I concede.'

Exclamations of relief and celebration immediately broke out all around. Esme threw her arms around Andrew; I hugged Ivy, then Ben. Were we a little hysterical? What would we think of this night when we looked back on it from our uncertain futures? What on earth were we doing? Ivy read the questions in my face before I spoke.

'It's right,' she said. 'I know it's right.'

'You're not doing it because of me, are you?' asked Ben at her side. 'As a chance to get me off the hook?'

'By putting all of us on it?' she grinned. 'A bit, if I'm honest. But mainly to put the balance right. Do you know what I mean?'

'I do.'

'Well said, darling.' I squeezed her arm.

'Right,' Andrew spoke to the room. 'We need to make plans. I suggest Donald and I take the body to the loch tonight.'

'And me.' Ben stepped forward.

'If you wish. Then tomorrow we walk to Newton Stewart and report him missing.'

'Ask at the railway station first and the hotel,' said Fiona. 'That's what you'd do if you were really looking for him.'

'Good idea.'

We're really doing this, I told myself. It's happening. What is it Bassanio says in *The Merchant of Venice*? 'To do a great right, do a little wrong.' There was no going back now. *I'm bound to these people forever*, I thought. *For as long as I live.*

That's when the phone rang.

43

IVY

The hills were still blanketed in snow and the water was a winding expanse of silver, tinged with soft pink from the dawn sky. At first light, we had all walked up to Bruce's stone to stare out at the loch and pay our last respects to Max Coyle, now lying in his final resting place somewhere in its silent depths. I shuddered to think of it and Ben, grim-eyed at my side, drew me to him without speaking. On my other side, Holly clutched my arm with her gloved hand, and I was glad to feel the living warmth of both of them. We were a solemn group, gathered together as the winter sun rose behind the clouds, breath misting in the freezing air, all our faces grave with thoughts of what we had done and what the days to come would bring.

The ringing phone last night had us all jumping out of our skins. A sound we hadn't heard for days, that we had wished for with varying degrees of impatience but which, just then, seemed like an invasion, an unwanted witness. We were all frozen to the spot until Andrew stirred himself and went into the hall to answer it. He was only gone a few minutes.

'Just the exchange,' he said as he came in. 'All the lines are back up now. That spares us a long walk tomorrow.'

'Yes, but it means we must raise the alarm tonight.' Fiona was thinking clearly, as always. 'Anything else would look suspicious.'

'Shouldn't the body be moved before we contact anyone?' asked Dorothy. 'What if the police come straight away?'

'The roads aren't clear yet. I can't imagine they'd try and get through before tomorrow. But we'll all breathe easier when it's done, I expect.' Andrew looked to Donald and Ben. 'I suggest we go now, if you agree?'

They followed him to the door. Thinking of what lay ahead for them out on the dark water, I sought out Ben's eyes. He gave me a little smile of reassurance that went straight to my heart.

As they moved off, Sonya spoke.

'If I was really looking for him, I'd phone home I guess, now that I can. Shall I do that whilst you're gone?'

It was generally agreed that she should. Then the three men donned waterproofs and went out into the freezing night. It was moonless and inky black. Through the window I could barely make them out as they walked up to the summer house. Straining my eyes, I watched until their shadows disappeared in the darkness.

Sonya's voice carried from the hall as she put through a call to her London house and we all fell silent, listening to her faultless performance. Curiosity, surprise, just enough concern and instructions that he be asked to get in touch if he arrived home.

'First base covered,' she called as she hung up. 'Esme, you should call the hotel in Newton Stewart next.'

'Would you prefer I do it, darling?' Holly asked her.

'No. I'll be fine.'

And she was. It was useful, in the circumstances, to have a house full of actors.

After that, we waited. Esme poured drinks and Jean went to the kitchen to heat some soup.

'It's a snell night. They'll need a warm when they get back.'

Holly sank into a sofa and pulled me down next to her.

'It's good that Ben offered to go,' she said. 'He's a good man.'

'Yes.' My heart swelled.

'I'm worried about Godfrey.'

I knew what she was thinking. He hadn't spoken since the phone rang. What was on his mind? Calling the police, confessing and putting an end to the whole thing? I'm ashamed to say that a little part of me wished he would. I pushed the thought away resolutely and called to him, indicating a chair at my side.

'Come and sit with us. They won't be long now.'

Once he was seated, Holly reached over and placed a hand on his.

'Are you all right?'

'That isn't important. My concern is for all of you.'

'We're fine.' Esme was a few feet away, with Ishbel. 'We'll all be fine.'

'Personally, I'm better than I've been for years.' Elliot shared a smile with Dorothy, attracting a few curious looks, but he didn't offer an explanation. ''Tis a far, far better thing we do and all that.'

'You do remember what happened to Sydney Carton?' Holly asked.

There was a beat as we registered it. Elliot laughed and Holly joined him and then we were all laughing and the sound rang through the house, sudden and comforting. The mood in the room shifted.

'We can do this,' said Dorothy and I believed her.

Standing above the loch in the chill morning air, I held on to that moment. It was unthinkable that Godfrey should face the hangman. An uneasy conscience was nothing compared to that. We would soon be back in our lives and all this would fade, would prick less as time passed. The disappearance of Max Coyle would be a sensation until it wasn't. Some mysteries are never solved. The world turns.

Esme had proposed, before we all went to bed last night, that we take a few moments together to acknowledge a life ended, whatever our individual feelings about it. I suggested Bruce's stone, so here we were. There were no speeches, no readings, just our silent thoughts. *There are worse places to lie forever,* I thought, looking out at the vast, beautiful landscape all around us. *Age-old rock and earth and we just pass through in the blink of an eye.*

'Penny for 'em,' said Ben softly.

'Mortality.' I held onto him even tighter.

'Better be getting back.' Elliot had been the most reluctant to attend and was clearly impatient to leave. He tugged at Dorothy's sleeve. 'The police will be phoning soon.'

'Do you think they will get through the snow today?' asked Godfrey.

Jean was on one side of him, Donald on the other. With their help, he had made it up the slope, insistent and determined.

'Unlikely,' Donald said. 'But maybe tomorrow.'

In the meantime they were beginning enquiries, they had told us. Max was officially a missing person now.

'Are you ready, Mr Clifford?' Jean took Godfrey's arm. 'Let's get you doon the brae.'

'Thank you.' He smiled at her. 'Do you think, considering the circumstances, that we might perhaps be on first name terms now?'

'I think that would be fine, Godfrey,' she replied simply.

They set off down the slope but Fiona, who was with them, lingered by the stone. Seeing me watching her, she nodded at the lichen-spotted words.

'A decisive end, it says. And here we are, still fighting, six hundred years later.'

Holly turned to Ben.

'Darling, it's icy in places. Be dashing and lend your manly arms to Ishbel and Esme.'

I could see she was burning to grill Fiona and needed rid of him so I threw him an apologetic look and chimed in.

'I won't be long.'

He surrendered with good grace. He was learning that's the simplest way with Holly. I waved him off and the interrogation began as soon as he was out of earshot.

'Have you heard from your friend now the phone is working?'

'I spoke to her late last night,' said Fiona softly. 'The police know who took it. They've been up there, questioning her. They think she took the whole stone across the border. No idea it broke in two.'

'What did she tell them?'

'That it was in a peat bog behind the croft and they were welcome to look for it.'

'Brave.'

'She is.'

'Are they making arrests?'

'No one so far. Kay reckons they're afraid of making martyrs.'

'Is it true?' I asked. 'Is it buried in a bog?'

Fiona's freckled face broke into a wide grin.

'It's buried, sure enough.'

Apart from the three of us, only Andrew was still on the hilltop. He was standing by a rough cairn of rugged grey rocks at the side of the main boulder, seemingly deep in thought. When Fiona spoke, he looked up and both Holly and me caught the look that passed between them. I saw realisation dawn in Holly's face as I jumped to my own conclusion.

'Andrew!' she exclaimed. 'You know all about it.'

His reply was a broad smile.

'You know it was here!'

'Of course. Donald told me straight after the young lady knocked on his door.'

'You dark horse!'

'That was why Donald came up to the patio before Max was murdered,' I said. 'To tell you Kay and the stone were safe away.'

The mischief in his eyes deepened. Holly registered it too.

'What?' she asked. 'What is it?'

'As Ivy said, Kay is safe and the stone is safe. Shall we go down?'

Holly clearly wasn't satisfied and looked to me for help but my mind was already making connections. Donald MacRae up at the crack of dawn on Boxing Day, down at the gates with a shovel in his hand. Andrew walking down this very hill to greet me at the loch side soon after. I looked at the mounds of rock and snow around the monument and thought how easily another stone could lie undiscovered in this remote spot for as long as was needed.

'Oh,' I gasped.

'What?' Holly demanded.

'Is it...?'

Fiona smiled at Andrew.

'I don't know what she's on about. Do you?'

'Haven't a clue.'

'Oh good heavens!' Holly had caught up. Her face was a picture. 'It's here—?'

'I don't know about you,' said Andrew, 'but I'm ready for my breakfast.'

'Did you—?'

'Famished,' said Fiona.

There was a beat. Then Holly looked from them to me and back again, her blue eyes sparkling with delight.

'Very well,' she beamed. 'Understood. But can I just say, how utterly wonderful!'

'And can I say,' I added, 'some secrets are an obligation, but some are a positive pleasure.'

We laughed then and there were hugs all round.

'Does Esme know?' asked Holly.

'Not yet. She's had enough to deal with. I didn't want to burden her further. But I'll tell her as soon as things settle down. And now, can we please get breakfast? Crime works up an appetite.'

As we followed him home, a flight of birds took off from the surface of the loch and flew over our heads with a rush of wings. I looked back at Bruce's stone, standing proud against the wide sky, and thought there was nowhere more fitting for even a small part of the Stone of Destiny to rest, till it could be made whole once again.

With Andrew and Fiona striding ahead, Holly linked her arm in mine.

'What an adventure!'

'That's one way of describing it.'

'"Have Yourself a Merry Little Christmas",' she sang in my ear.

'Behave.'

'You know I never will.'

'I know.'

She gave a deep, satisfied chuckle.

'What larks, darling. Here's to many more.'

'Oh, Dame Elspeth,' I told her happily. 'I don't doubt that for a minute.'

APPENDIX

In the early hours of Christmas Day 1950, four Scottish students from Glasgow University removed the Stone of Destiny from Westminster Abbey. Whilst they were pulling it out from under the Coronation Chair, the stone broke into two pieces. The larger part was buried in a Kent field by Ian Hamilton, Gavin Vernon and Alan Stuart. The smaller part was driven north by Kay Matheson. There are differing stories of exactly where she left it. Perhaps with a friend in Birmingham, perhaps on her parents' croft in the Highlands.

There was an outcry and major investigation and search but it was unsuccessful.

On 11 April 1951, the repaired stone was left on the altar of the ruined Arbroath Abbey and the authorities were informed of its whereabouts. It was then returned to Westminster. No arrests were made.

On 15 November 1996, the Stone of Destiny was formally returned to Scotland.

For the purposes of my story, I have taken the stone to Loch Trool in Dumfries and Galloway. I hope Robert the Bruce, Kay, Ian, Gavin, Alan and *clach-na-cinneamhain* itself will forgive me.

ACKNOWLEDGEMENTS

With gratitude to everyone at Honno Press, especially my editor Janet Thomas, for her expert guidance and good humour.

Love and thanks, as always, to Mark, for the floor plans of Black Gairy, the field trips and conversations, for the patience, support and encouragement.

Big hugs to the loyal friends who read the proofs and endorsed the book.

Finally, thank you to all the wonderful whodunnit writers who have given me a lifetime of joyous reading and provided the inspiration for Holly and Ivy's adventures. I am so happy to be carrying on the tradition.

ABOUT HONNO

Honno Welsh Women's Press was set up in 1986 by a group of women who felt strongly that women in Wales needed wider opportunities to see their writing in print and to become involved in the publishing process. Our aim is to develop the writing talents of women in Wales, give them new and exciting opportunities to see their work published and often to give them their first 'break' as a writer.

Honno is registered as a community co-operative. Any profit that Honno makes is invested in the publishing programme. Women from Wales and around the world have expressed their support for Honno. Each supporter has a vote at the Annual General Meeting. For more information and to buy our publications, please visit our website www.honno.co.uk or email us on post@honno.co.uk.

Honno
D41, Hugh Owen Building,
Aberystwyth University,
Aberystwyth,
Ceredigion,
SY23 3DY.

We are very grateful for the support of
all our Honno Friends.